THE ORANGE-TREE PLOT

THE ORANGE TREE PLOT

— A NOVEL —

Cynthia Harrod-Eagles

SIDGWICK & JACKSON

LONDON

First published in Great Britain by Sidgwick & Jackson Limited

Copyright © Cynthia Harrod-Eagles, 1989

ISBN 0-283-99966-7

Typeset by Hewer Text Composition Services, Edinburgh
Printed by Billing & Sons Ltd, Worcester
for Sidgwick & Jackson Limited
1 Tavistock Chambers, Bloomsbury Way
London WC1A 2SG

Chapter One

It was one thing, Eugenie thought, to escape death under the blade of the guillotine at the hands of Robespierre's Revolutionary Tribunal, and one could not but be grateful and thank *le bon Dieu* for one's deliverance; but another to go on being grateful, and to maintain a glad heart in the face of a prolonged crossing of the aptly named English Channel – for who but the English would wish to lay claim to a place so lashed with rain, so tormented by gales and storms, above all so *cold*?

Eugenie, who had been given at her birth the resounding names of Eugenie Marie Christine Hélène d'Issy-Sable, and has been baptised by the Bishop of Paris himself in the ancient font of Notre Dame de Paris; on whose behalf the Devil and his works had been renounced by none other than Madame Adelaide, the King's aged aunt; who had cut her teeth upon the famous d'Issy Ruby, a gigantic stone of flawless clarity, which rested like a great drop of heart's blood in the ring upon the signet finger of her father, the Comte de Talcy; and who at the age of five had been given her own household of twelve servants – this same Eugenie first set foot on English soil possessed of nothing but the clothes she stood up in, and accompanied by a single maid, the faithful Marie Meunier.

For the first fifteen years of her life, Eugenie had seemed to lead a charmed existence. Her father was a rich and handsome man, last representative of an old and noble line, and was possessed of a large and undisputed inheritance. Talcy itself was a small village in the Touraine. There was a fifteenth-century château, several farms, and a fine vineyard, all belonging to the Count, who visited them as infrequently as possible, preferring the life of Paris and Versailles. He also owned several streets of houses in the Quartier Écosse; a mine in the department of Oise, to the north, and another, larger, in the Ruhr valley; and a sugar plantation in Martinique which he had never seen.

His wife, Marie-Christine de Sable, united beauty with a large dowry, and brought both to her husband on their marriage, along with sixteen quarterings to impale with his own overcrowded arms. They sometimes disputed in a friendly manner as to whose family was the most ancient and venerable, happy in the knowledge that the honours were equal, and that, though their marriage had been arranged for them, they had had the great good fortune to fall devotedly in love at first sight. The Comtesse was a little disappointed when her first child proved to be a girl, but accepted her husband's assurances that the next would certainly be a boy, and that he had always had a secret longing for a daughter.

The Comtesse was glad to be comforted. She came from that strange region in the south-west of France called simply *Les Landes*, a flat and marshy place where the great Atlantic rollers sigh ceaselessly, and expire at the end of their long journey upon a sandy shore as straight as a rule, divided from the land only by low dunes colonised by coarse marram and wild lupins, and a string of shallow lagoons. Here her family had bred cattle for the last four hundred years, tough little black creatures with long straight horns, whose tempers were fierce, but whose meat was seemingly sweeter for the salt of the grass they grazed. The de Sable fortune had always been in their land and in their cattle, and such a family needs sons. It had been bred into Marie-Christine's bones that a man must have male children, and that the wife who gives him girls is failing in her duty.

Her husband's novel approach therefore seemed to her a revelation, a symptom of the more kindly and liberal attitude generated by the ease of life in the soft, green north, compared with that of the spare and gale-swept country of her birth. When Eugenie was six months old, the Comtesse went, with her husband's permission, to visit her family, to explain to them that dear de Talcy was not at all disappointed with his daughter. It was autumn, and a cold and wet one. Marie-Christine returned to Paris mentally refreshed, but fatally infected with that wasting disease of the lungs which seems to favour marshy regions. By Christmas she was dead, and nine-month-old Eugenie was motherless.

It was not to be supposed that the young and vigorous Comte with only a daughter to follow him would not marry again, and those who loved Eugenie – and already they were many – prepared to see her ousted from her father's affections by a new stepmother and a string of half-brothers. But months, and then years passed, the Comte did not remarry, and Eugenie remained his heart's treasure. Nothing was too good for her: she must have the finest apartments in the Hotel de Talcy on the Isle de St Louis, a large retinue of hand-picked servants, the finest food, the finest clothes. As she grew she was given also the best tutors, just as if she had been a boy, to train her mind and body to perfection, and her own personal chaplain and confessor to take care of her soul.

But she was not left alone with her servants. Her father visited her daily, played with her, talked to her, even encouraged her to accompany him on walks and rides. Thus it was, when she wailed with teething pains, that it was her father's hand which soothed her hot face, and it was upon the d'Issy Ruby that she clamped her gums for relief. When she was only three, he took her up on the front of his saddle to ride in the woods around Versailles. When she was five, he taught her to skate on the frozen ponds at Compiègne, and had made for her a special skating dress of scarlet velvet trimmed with white ermine. And on her ninth birthday he gave her an exquisite child-sized calèche – with gilded scrollwork, painted panels, and a pair of white ponies in jewelled harnesses – in which she could be seen driving herself every Sunday along the fashionable carriageways of the Bois de Boulogne.

Her grandmother's sister, the aged Comtesse de Narrandais, the only relative she had on her father's side, issued frequent and stern warnings about the likely consequences of such indulgence, and took her away from her father to her country house in Thierry as often as he would permit. Madame de Narrandais, in her distant girlhood, had been sent to be educated in the household of an English earl, and was crustily reverential towards all things English, particularly their stern and practical attitude to their children. At the house in Thierry little Eugenie ate plain food, went for sedate walks, practised long upon the harpsichord, and spent even longer hours learning to sew. Plain hemming, delicate embroidery, gros point, petit point, tapestry work, knotting, dressmaking – all were mastered under the supervision of her great-aunt, whose sharp eyes watched her for any sign of pride or arrogance.

But Eugenie, in spite of everything, remained relentlessly unspoiled. She received every attention with wonder, gratitude and love, and paid it back with interest. Even Madame de Narrandais was forced to admit that the child had a sweet and pliable nature, and was more than once seen to embrace her little great-niece and bid her goodnight with what her elderly maid Solange could only describe in amazement as a smile.

When she was fifteen her father, with his aunt's assistance, brought Eugenie out into society, and she was presented at Versailles. The pretty little Queen was no longer the heedless girl she had been when she first came from Austria: she had settled down, had come to love her husband, and had given him a number of children, of whom three had survived. At the time of Eugenie's presentation in the March of 1789, the eight-year-old Dauphin was giving his parents great anxiety on account of his health, but still the Queen found time to smile and make a pleasant little joke to set Eugenie at ease. Afterwards there followed the usual round of balls and assemblies and visits to the theatre and the opera, and the Comte de Talcy had the pleasure of seeing his daughter the most feted *debutante* of the season, and the pain of knowing that he must soon arrange her marriage to some utterly unworthy young man – for in the face of Eugenie's perfections, every young man must be unworthy.

But the golden times, which they had assumed would go on for ever, were rapidly coming to an end. In May 1789 came the long-awaited convening of the Estates General – an extraordinary assembly, last called a hundred and seventy-five years before, and called now only because long mismanagement and the disastrous American wars had left the country poised perilously on the edge of bankruptcy. With a few exceptions, the wealth of the country was all in the hands of the middle ranks, while the power remained with the nobility. The middle ranks were seething with discontent and the determination to remedy the injustice, as they saw it. The three Estates met at Versailles, the First and Second Estates – the nobles and the clergy – with the firm intention of clinging on to their ancient privilege, and the Third Estate – the bourgeoisie, largely represented by lawyers – with the firm intention of wresting it from them.

On the fourth of June, the Dauphin died of his long-suffered illness, and the ancient title passed to his little brother, the Duc de Normandie. The King and Queen were plunged into grief. The Court went into mourning and the untroubled gaiety of Versailles ended for ever, for in July the Third Estate proclaimed itself to be the only true representative of the people of France, and renamed itself the National Assembly. Under its influence, a mob stormed and seized the old fortress prison of the Bastille, forcing the King to acknowledge the new order.

From that moment, everything else that happened was inevitable, as Eugenie could see on looking back, though at the time she, like everyone else caught in her position, had hoped from day to day that the horrors would stop and that life would settle down again as it had used to be. One by one the King's powers were taken from him, until he and his family were no better than prisoners in the Tuileries. Their attempted escape to Austria, foiled at the very last moment when they were only a few miles from safety, led to real imprisonment in the Temple, and at last, inevitably, to the horror and sacrilege of their execution.

Paris descended, reeling, through the insanity of the September Massacres to rule by the Revolutionary Tribunal and the guillotine. Normality fled: the Terror began. Any citizen, great or humble, might suddenly find himself denounced by his neighbour for a lack of revolutionary fervour and dragged off to his execution. No defence was allowed: to be arrested was to be condemned, and few who rattled off in the tumbrels to the Place de la Révolution understood what they had done to bring this upon themselves.

Through all the death throes of the old order, de Talcy had managed, just, to keep his footing. In the beginning he had been one of those who had favoured a measure of reform, and at the time of the National Assembly he had been considered a radical. All the same, as the radicals of one government became the reactionaries of the next, de Talcy found his position increasingly difficult. His title and much of his property had been seized, and from the moment of the storming of the Bastille, when the members of the aristocracy began slipping out of France, fleeing to places of safety with as much of their wealth as they could carry, he was aware that he was under suspicion for having helped a number of old friends to escape.

He had protected Eugenie as much as possible from the events which were the milestones of what should have been her carefree years, but he had brought her up to be an intelligent companion, and could not keep her wholly in the dark. When her great-aunt de Narrandais was executed, Eugenie, pale with tears and determination, insisted on helping her father. ·

'They guillotined her like a common criminal,' she cried hotly. 'They even executed poor Solange, who could not by any sane person be considered guilty of any crime! Papa, we must do all we can to oppose them.'

'My love, there is very little we can do,' de Talcy said sadly.

'We can help others to leave France,' Eugenie said. 'Everyone who escapes the guillotine strikes a blow for freedom and sanity.'

De Talcy was reluctant. 'It will be dangerous. Already I am being watched.'

Eugenie saw with alarm how grey he had grown of late. He was forty-seven, but looked ten years older. She slipped her hand in his and smiled comfortingly. 'I can help you, Papa. There are many things I can do which you cannot. If you are watched, I may slip under their guard.'

So for six months they had worked together, building up a network of secret channels along which those most desperately in need could be passed to safety. Some were aristocrats, who rewarded the de Talcys richly with money and jewels; others were of the lower orders, whose thanks were only words, or the grateful press of a hand. The strain told on them both, and they were aware that sooner or later they must make their own escape, before the suspicions of the authorities hardened into certainty. Then in March 1794, Louis Eugene Hector Christian d'Issy, fourteenth Comte de Talcy, suffered a stroke while asleep in his own bed, and went peacefully and painlessly to join his ancestors in Paradise.

Eugenie hardly had the leisure to mourn her father. His death, she felt sure, had alone prevented his arrest, and had left her with the immediate necessity of removing herself from the eye of Robespierre's agents. She ought, she knew, to leave France at once, but there were many matters still in hand which she was loth to leave unfinished, and it was not until the end of April that she finally passed herself, accompanied by her maid Marie, her old nurse, a footman, two trunks of clothes, and a small leather-bound trunk containing the bulk of d'Issy jewels which her father had managed to keep hidden, down the well-worn escape route towards England.

Unfortunately, the route had become a little too well worn. Alarm and pursuit immediately followed their quitting of Paris, and at Abbeville the party split in the hope of foiling the trail, intending to meet up again at St Omer, where the boat would be waiting. At St Omer, Eugenie and Marie found not only that the other servants and the luggage had not arrived, but that the boat had already sailed. They laid up in hiding for a day, but the nurse and the footman did not appear, and at length Eugenie was forced to hire the only other available sailing vessel with the last of her gold, and she and Marie embarked for England with nothing but a cloak bag containing necessities for the journey.

They met foul weather as soon as they cleared the harbour bar, and the little boat, which had intended to land at a small inlet on the Kent coast, was driven down the Channel by a storm which Eugenie was sure had its origins in the frozen steppes of Russia. The two women, wracked by nausea and terror, said their last prayers and then clung to each other, wondering if the worst the Revolutionary Tribunal could have done to them would not be better than this. The guillotine was at least quick, and Eugenie, as her stomach seemed to be trying to force its way out through the top of her head, thought she might even be glad to be rid of the latter. Twenty-four hours later, and twenty hours after the two women were positive they could bear it not a moment longer, the storm blew itself out, and the boat was able to make landfall near Selsey. They had reached England and safety – but what an England! The storm had passed, but the wind was still strong, the sky a uniform blanket of tearing grey clouds, and the rain continuous, though fluctuating in cold malice towards the bare and inhospitable landscape in which they found themselves. And what safety, Eugenie wondered? She had envisaged herself arriving unruffled, if interestingly pale, with luggage, servants and jewels, to be whisked away in a comfortable carriage to London and reunion with some of those *émigrés* whom she and Papa had helped and who would surely be grateful and eager to help her settle down in her country of adoption.

She was realist enough to know that a very different reception would await her, penniless and unprotected as she was. She had no idea where to go or what to do. If her servants had sailed before her in the boat she had intended to take, they might be waiting for her somewhere in Kent; on the other hand, the same storm might have blown them, too, off course, or even sunk them altogether. If, as seemed more likely, they had not left France, there was no knowing when they would be able to do so, or where they might land. It seemed best, therefore, as she agreed with Marie, to try to make their way to London. She knew that many of the *émigrés* had settled in a village on the outskirts of London called Brompton. This village had often been spoken of amongst them, and if Pierre and old Nana did manage to get to England, they would surely remember the name. In Brompton there would be someone to help her. Eugenie had complete faith in her countrymen. Exiles in a foreign land would naturally band together to help one another.

The immediate imperative was to seek shelter from the

rain, and information as to their whereabouts. There was but one track leading from the shore where they had landed, and they took it, Eugenie setting the pace, and Marie walking behind, carrying the cloak bag which contained their clean underlinen, hairbrushes and toothbrushes. The only things of value Eugenie now possessed were around her neck: a string of pearls which had been her mother's, and a gold cross and chain.

'I must part with them, I suppose,' she said to Marie mournfully. 'But perhaps I may pledge them, and redeem them later.' The notion cheered her, and she walked on determinedly, head down against the driving rain. Two miles inland, they came to a tiny village, no more than a handful of cottages, all sealed tight against the weather. 'We must knock at a door, and ask for directions,' Eugenie said, trembling a little, for the idea was novel, and a little alarming. 'Thank heaven Papa insisted that I should learn English.'

'Thank heaven, mademoiselle, that you worked hard at your studies,' Marie said as fervently as shortness of breath would allow. The gratitude was premature. Prolonged knocking at the first cottage produced no answer at all. Either all within were deaf, or asleep, or, as seemed more likely, they had no intention of opening the door to strangers. The second cottage, however, produced an old man, the creases of whose face were filled with white whiskers, like a light snowfall on ploughed land. He stared at them in wonder, and it took a very long time to make him understand their request for information, and for them to understand his answers, spoken as they were in a quavering voice and an impenetrable country accent.

London, they learnt at last, was some seventy miles off. The nearest town was Chichester, which was another five or six miles along this road, and from there coaches went to London, he could not say when, nor how long the journey took, nor how much it cost. Such things seemed far out of his realm of experience; indeed, Eugenie doubted if he understood that they had come from France. To such a man, a village ten miles off would be foreign country enough. This village, he told them, was called Norton. No, there was no inn in the village, nor any kind of hostelry any closer than Chichester, nor any house where gentryfolk lived. To Chichester, then, it was plain they must go: there was no shelter here for them. They thanked the man and walked on, as he stood at his door watching them, shaking his head slowly from side to side in wonder and disbelief that such things could be.

The road seemed very long, and it was late when they reached the outskirts of Chichester, their only consolation being that the rain stopped and the clouds parted towards the end of their journey, to give them the benefit of a gibbous moon. It was a new experience for Eugenie, to be turned away from the first inn they came to, apostrophised as a gypsy, and no better than she ought. The second was little more than an alehouse: one tiny parlour below, where three old men sat silently in a row on a bench, with wooden piggins in their hands, two rooms above, and an attic for the servants. Here they had better luck. The landlady, though rough-looking, seemed quick witted, and a decent sort. She sympathised with their plight, tutted over the ruin of their shoes and hems, and agreed to give them a bed for the night and a meal in exchange for the gold cross and chain.

'Not that I hold with popery and idolatry,' she added sternly, 'but there, I don't suppose you can help it, being foreigners. Lord, what terrible things are going on over there, to be sure!' And seeing that they were ready to drop, she shooed them up the narrow, precipitous stairs and showed them into the bedroom, where she put a light to the fire that was laid there, tutted over its slow and smoky beginnings, and left them to take off their wraps.

The two women were too exhausted to speak. Marie automatically bent to take off Eugenie's shoes, but Eugenie gently pushed her away, and saw to them herself. The fire was crackling now, though still giving off more smoke than heat. She supposed it had been laid some time, and had got damp from rain falling down the chimney. The little room smelled stale, and the sheets on the bed looked none too clean, but in their present state it was near to heaven. A little while later the landlady appeared again with a tray on which were two bowls of hot soup, a mess of beans, some cold meat, which proved to be mutton, and a loaf of bread. She set down the tray, poked the fire, and picked up the two pairs of shoes which Eugenie had set down in the fender, shaking her head over them.

'Lord, what a shame to walk so far in these poor things! It's clear you're gentryfolk in your own country, or you'd have been better shod for walking. I'll take them down to the kitchen and dry them for you, though I doubt they'll ever be worth wearing again. Still,' she added, giving them a curious look, 'beggars can't be choosers, can they?'

When they were alone again, Marie began to cry quietly. 'Oh mademoiselle, that it should come to this! For myself I do not mind, but that you should be called a beggar by a common tavernwoman!'

Eugenie felt tears prickling in her own eyes, but blinked them back, trying for a cheerful tone. 'Just at the moment, dear Marie, we are beggars, or very near. But never mind. All will be well again, once we get to London. Now, let us eat this food which the good woman has brought us. I for one am very hungry, and the soup smells good.'

Marie sniffed dismally. 'Not as good as even I could make, mademoiselle, and I'm a lady's maid. The English don't understand about food.'

Eugenie laughed. 'Oh Marie, what do you know about England? You have only been here one day. Here, take some bread, and eat.'

By the time they had cleared the tray, and the fire had burned up, they both felt better, only very weary and longing for sleep; but they knelt together to give thanks to God and the Blessed Lady, and to St Anthony the patron of travellers for their deliverance so far, before taking off their dresses and crawling, too tired to be suspicious, between the grubby sheets. The ancient mattress was as lumpy as a cobbled street, but they were asleep long before its shortcomings could be fully appreciated.

The landlady's good will extended to breakfast the next morning: some thick slices of fat pork belly fried in oatmeal, a dish of eggs, fresh bread, and a quart of ale. Marie eyed the latter indignantly, and asked for coffee for her lady, at which the landlady gave an incredulous smile and shook her head. Whether she was indicating that coffee was not to be found in such an establishment as this, or that it was not to be had for the price of a gold cross and chain, was uncertain, but the negative was decided, and Eugenie stilled her maid with a look and poured herself some ale.

'You'll be making for London then, I suppose?' the good woman said, stooping to throw a few more faggots on the fire. Eugenie agreed. 'You'll not walk all the way in those shoes,' the landlady concluded. 'How do you mean to get on?'

'I had hoped we might be able to buy places on the stagecoach,' Eugenie said. 'There is a coach to London, is there not?'

'Oh, aye, it goes from the Crown every day.' The shrewd eyes narrowed. 'But you've no money, have you?'

'I have still my mother's pearls,' Eugenie said, her fingers going automatically to her throat. 'I thought perhaps they would let me pledge them against the tickets.'

'What, the coaching company? Oh no, miss, you're adrift there! It's ready money for them or nothing,' said the woman, seeming amused.

'Then I suppose I must sell them,' Eugenie said sadly. The landlady eyed her thoughtfully.

'Aye, but you can't just go to a shop in the town and sell them. You'd be cheated, sure as you sit there, you being a foreigner and all – even if they'd take them.

They might think you'd stolen them, and send for the magistrate.'

Eugenie looked alarmed. 'Then what must I do?'

'I'll tell you what – which is more than I'd do for anyone else, but I've taken a liking to you, miss, and I want to help you – you may leave them pearls with me. I'll give you a price for them, and keep 'em safe here, and when you get to London and find your friends, why, you can send for 'em again.'

Marie, not understanding what was being said, but mis-liking the look in the woman's eye, hissed imperatively at Eugenie, 'Qu'est-ce qu'elle dit?' Eugenie translated. Marie exclaimed, 'But she will cheat you, mademoiselle, of a certainty.'

'Of course,' said the landlady, as if on cue, 'I couldn't give you a great deal for them – I don't keep much money in the house, in case of robbers – but it's better than losing them altogether, isn't it?'

To Marie, Eugenie said, 'I can't help it, Marie. It is true, what she says. Anyone in the town might cheat me, and I would never see my dear mama's pearls again. It is better I let her have them. There is a chance then I may be able to redeem them.' And to the landlady she said, 'Very well, madame. I am grateful to you, and I will send for them again as soon as I reach London.'

'You do that, miss,' said the landlady; and so well pleased was she with her transaction that she even arranged for her potboy to take the two women to the Crown on the back of the cart on his way to market. Eugenie knew nothing about English money, and had no way of knowing whether the amount she had been given was reasonable or derisory. She soon learnt that it was not, at any rate, sufficient to buy two tickets to London: for the amount in her hand, she was told at the Crown, she and her maid could be carried only as far as Kingston. The glazed indifference in the eyes of the man with his hand poised over the waybill dissuaded her from asking what she must do then. She drew on a mantle of dignity and said, 'Please take us, then, as far as you can.'

'Nothing to do with me, miss. I just make up the 'bills. Coach leaves at eleven o'clock *prompt*.'

Eugenie nodded and led her maid outside, and tried not to let her lip tremble. All the money was gone. She had parted with her mother's pearls. The coach would deposit them still many miles from their destination, and they had not the means to pay for food or lodgings. People spoke harshly to her, looked at her with indifferent eyes, cared nothing for what happened to her. She was a stranger in a foreign land, and her father was dead, and she was only nineteen years old.

Then she saw Marie looking at her with a mixture of distress and expectation. Marie loved her and cared for her, but depended on her not only for her livelihood but for guidance. Marie could not speak English, nor make a decision on her own behalf, and her case was therefore worse than Eugenie's. It was a bracing thought. Eugenie conjured up a smile, and if it was a little shaky, still it did them both good.

'What a pretty town this is,' she said brightly. 'And the rain has stopped, and the sun is trying the break through the clouds. Shall we walk a little, Marie, and look around us? And perhaps we may find some place to sit down. The time will pass very quickly.'

Chapter Two

Eugenie had need of all her resolution to remain cheerful. The evening of her second day on English soil found her and her maid still ten miles from London, hungry, tired, and completely destitute. The stage-coach had set them down in the middle of Kingston, and there seemed no choice but to begin to walk the rest of the way to London, and hope that some passing farm vehicle or carrier's cart would offer to take them up.

Kingston, though a popular watering place, was but a small town, and having set off on the London road, the two women were soon clear of the town proper. The houses thinned out, and though they continued to pass smartly-kept properties here and there to either side of the road, the gaps between them lengthened, and it was clear they would soon be in open countryside. Eugenie had never ceased to listen for the sound of hooves, and they had not gone more than a mile when she heard what sounded like a gentleman's sporting vehicle coming up fast behind them. She glanced back, and saw that it was in fact a smart curricle, drawn by a pair of fine bays and driven by a gentleman in a white driving coat, with his groom behind.

'Oh, that is no use to us,' she muttered, drawing Marie off the road to let it pass. It hurtled down towards them at spanking pace, and too late Eugenie saw that they were standing perilously near to a large puddle left by the recent rains in an inequality of the road's surface. The light was reflecting on the surface of the puddle, and Eugenie felt sure that the driver would slow for it, but he did not. The vehicle dashed past, sending a sheet of muddy water over the two women, and Eugenie, who caught the brunt of it, let out a yelp of mingled anguish and rage.

This the driver evidently heard: he checked his pair and turned his head to look back. Eugenie saw a handsome, proud face, whose fine lips seemed curved in an expression of permanent haughtiness. For a moment their eyes met. That the gentleman took in the situation at a glance she had no doubt, but the next instant she saw him shrug indifferently and send his team dashing on.

'Oh!' she cried out in exasperation, and stamped her sodden foot in helpless fury. 'That beast! That imbecile! That – that – ' No epithet she was able to supply would have been sufficient to the case. 'If ever I meet him again, what will I not say to him!' But then she caught Marie's eye, and saw how damp and dishevelled she looked, and considered how unlikely it was that she should ever be in a position to berate a gentleman of such obvious affluence. It was a depressing thought.

Marie was clearly in no state to walk any further that day: apart from the fact that she was exhausted, her light shoes were in a worse condition than Eugenie's, and the sole was almost off one of them. A little further up the road there was a cottage: small, but modern-built, neat and handsome, evidently the dwelling of a person of means. Though it went against the grain to beg, Eugenie told herself she could no longer afford such fine feelings, and comforted herself that it was for Marie's sake more than her own. Taking the cloak bag from Marie's limp hand, she urged her along the last hundred yards, opened the wicket gate and determinedly marched her up the garden path.

A fine evening had succeeded the storms of the previous

days, and the sun was setting in a clear sky, a circumstance she hoped would sweeten the temper of the inhabitants of the cottage. Her knock upon the door aroused a tumult of barking from somewhere behind the house, but no other reply. After a while she knocked again, and at last a window to the side of the door opened, and a servant looked out. Eugenie watched, distressed, as the seemingly inevitable suspicion and hostility darkened the round cheerful face.

'What do you mean by knocking at the front door like that? What do you want?'

'Is your master at home, or your mistress?' Eugenie asked wearily, striving for as English a pronunciation as possible. The frown deepened.

'Who are you? No one from hereabouts knocks at the front door. In any case, it won't open – swollen up with all this damp. I warn you, if you're beggars, you can take yourselves off at once, for you'll get nothing here. We've dogs out the back, and I can let 'em loose in a moment.'

'No, we are not beggars,' Eugenie said. 'I wish to speak to your master. Is he at home?'

'Well, you look like beggars to me,' the woman said, though a little less harshly. 'And you speak funny, like a Dutchman.'

At that moment an upstairs window opened, and a young woman poked her head out and looked down, calling, 'What is it, Meg? Who are they?'

The servant craned her head upwards, now at a distinct disadvantage, and said, 'Beggars, ma'am, or gypsies. I've told them to be off.'

Eugenie, seeing that the face looking down upon her did not belong to a servant, and was benign in expression, stepped back to show herself more fully and said, 'Madame, I appeal to your kindness. We are not beggars, though we must appear so to your good servant. We have but yesterday arrived in England from France.'

The young woman's face brightened at once. 'From

France? What, are you emigrants, fleeing for your lives from bloodthirsty revolutionaries?'

'Now, ma'am,' said the servant warningly, but the young face above sparkled with excitement.

'Oh tush, Meg, this is the most exciting thing that has happened since the bull escaped from Upper Six Acres! I have been almost dead from boredom this age past! Do let the poor creatures in. You must be tired and hungry, mademoiselle,' she added to Eugenie.

'Yes, madame, we are, and beg the favour of a little food, and shelter for the night in some outhouse or barn,' Eugenie said.

'Oh you bold thing!' Meg cried, unwinding her neck to glare at Eugenie. 'I knew you was a beggar all along! Don't you listen to her, Miss Amabel. I'll set the dogs on them if they won't go.'

'Nonsense, Meg; don't you see the poor things need help? Take them into the kitchen, and I'll be down direct-ly!' And the casement was snapped closed on any further argument. Eugenie felt Marie sway with weariness, and automatically reached out an arm to support her, which seemed in some way to reassure the servant.

'Round the back, then,' she said, gesturing with her head, and then withdrew it and closed the window firmly.

A few moments later, the two fugitives were seated gratefully on a long settle beside the fireplace of a neat and cosy kitchen. Opposite them was a high-backed wooden chair with a patchwork cushion on its seat, on which a fat grey tabby cat disdained to wake from its doze on their account. A large black kettle was singing quietly at the back of the fire; a tall dresser in the corner was stacked with well-polished pewter and china; and on the scrubbed kitchen table a basket of mending showed how the occupant had been busying herself before their arrival.

The inner door of the kitchen opened, and the young woman of the house bounced through it, revealing her-self to be a plump and healthy girl of Eugenie's age, or

20

perhaps a little younger, with a pretty, good-humoured face, yellow curls elaborately dressed, and a high-waisted gown of sky-blue muslin which Eugenie thought hideous but which was evidently intended to be fashionable and smart.

'I am so glad you have come,' she cried as she advanced across the flagged kitchen floor. 'You cannot think how dull I have been, for *my husband* – ' she invested those words with a great significance and pride ' – is gone to London for the night, and I have no one to talk to, except Meg here, who is *so* disagreeable!' She bestowed on the servant a smile which robbed the words of any sting. 'You must be hungry, you poor things. Meg, would you get them some food – whatever is the quickest to prepare – and something to drink. Would you like some milk? Or, no, wait, a glass of wine would do you much more good, I am persuaded.'

'Now Miss Amabel – ' Meg protested.

'Oh, tush, Meg, I know what I'm about. The master's claret will be just the thing.' She turned to Eugenie with a smile. 'It is real French claret,' she said ingenuously. 'That will make you feel at home, won't it?'

Eugenie hardly knew whether to laugh or cry, but it was impossible to be offended by this amiable creature who was so like a merry child that she made Eugenie feel positively old by comparison. While Meg grudgingly began to prepare food, the young woman pattered about collecting a bottle and glasses, and then proved to be unable to open the bottle. Marie got up silently and took it from her, removing herself to the other side of the table with Meg to establish her status. She had not understood much of what was said, but she was sure that the young mistress of the house had thoroughly mistaken Eugenie's condition, or she would not have received her in the kitchen, which was quite improper for one of her rank. Meg glanced at her, and then moved aside to make room, understanding the gesture at once.

Relieved of her task, the young woman lifted the cat from the seat of the chair, sat down opposite Eugenie, and placed it on her lap. The cat gave her an offended look, jumped down, and stalked off to glare the kitchen door into opening for it.

'Now,' she said with a cheerful smile, 'what must I call you? I am Amabel Spender – no,' she blushed rosily, 'I mean Amabel McKendrick, Mrs James McKendrick. How foolish of me! But I have only been married six weeks, and I keep forgetting. Even Meg forgets and calls me Miss Amabel – she was my nurse, you know, when I lived at home with Papa and Mama and the darling boys.' She sighed. 'I do miss them all so much. There was always something happening, and noise and cheerfulness, and though I love James – Mr McKendrick – dearly, he is often from home, and then it is so very quiet and dull.' She intercepted a look from her servant, and smiled guiltily. 'Meg says I chatter too much. She says my tongue runs on wheels, but I was always the same way. Mama too – Papa says that when we two get together, there is no making oneself heard! Oh – how I miss them! But James – Mr McKendrick, I mean – is such a love! He is a lawyer, you know, and he is going to be very important one day. He has just been made Mr Spennilow's partner. I went into Kingston last week on purpose to see it written up on the office door, and it looked so very nice! Spennilow and McKendrick, Attorneys at Law, of The High Street, Kingston-upon-Thames. Doesn't that sound splendid? I longed to tell all the people passing by that he was my husband, but of course I did not, for he likes me to be very proper. Everyone knows him in Kingston, and so you see, one must be careful never to offend. And besides, my maid was with me, and she was such a cross old thing, always frowning at me in such a forbidding way. I was forced to give her her notice at last, and James was rather cross with me, but I said to him that there was no bearing her, and she was not very good at dressing hair either.

'Will you drink a little more wine? The colour is coming back to your cheeks at last. Your friend does not speak English, does she? But how very well you speak it, mademoiselle, quite like an English person, except, of course, for your accent, though many people think a French accent quite pretty. My friend Sally Heppel, who was at school with me – Mrs Barrington's Academy for Young Ladies in Richmond, you know – she is Mrs Charles Ottershaw now, and she has a French maid, though Meg thinks she is no more French than I am, and simply assumes the accent because French maids are paid more. But of course,' blushing again, 'I can tell that your accent is *quite* genuine. But you have not told me your name. I am quite longing to hear your story, if you will give yourself the trouble of telling it to me.'

The young woman paused for breath at last, and cocked an enquiring look at Eugenie, who thought she looked very much like a small and recently fledged bird.

'My name is Eugenie Marie Christine Hélène d'Issy-Sable,' she began, but got no further.

'And your friend?' nodding towards the table.

'She is Marie Meunier. But she is not – '

'Oh, that is very much easier to remember. So many Frenchwomen are called Marie, aren't they? May I call you Eugenie? I shall never be able to remember the rest. And you have come from Paris, you say? Mama went there on her honeymoon in '46, you know. I should so love to go there, but James says there will be no going abroad now until the war is over, and who knows how long that will be? And there are such stories being told about Paris, they quite make one's blood curdle! Are you indeed fleeing the revolutionaries? What is that wicked man's name? Robespierre, isn't it? And your luggage, what happened to that?'

'It was lost,' Eugenie said, resigning herself to the realisation that only short sentences had any chance of completion with this excitable young woman.

'And now you have nothing in the world but the clothes you stand up in!' She clasped her hands together in rapture. 'Oh, that is so very exciting!'

'I doubt the young woman don't find it exciting. How you do run on, Miss Amabel!' said Meg sternly.

Amabel looked contrite. 'Oh no, I didn't mean – how awful of me! I am so sorry. But such exciting things have happened to you, quite like in a novel, and nothing at all has ever happened to me, except for falling in love with Mr McKendrick, although I dare say I would have married him even if I hadn't fallen in love, for Papa said it was a good match, and I think it is every young woman's duty to marry as well as she can, don't you? You are not married? But I suppose it must have been difficult to think about weddings in the middle of a revolution. Mama and I took six months to prepare for my wedding, and we went to the best warehouse in London for my clothes. I'm afraid your gown has suffered sadly from the journey,' she added with a glance at Eugenie's hem. 'Tell me, do all Frenchwomen wear black?'

'We are in mourning,' Eugenie said gently. 'My father died two months ago.'

Amabel blushed scarlet with mortification, and Meg thrust herself nobly into the breach, bustling around the table and saying loudly, 'Now then, Miss Amabel, let the young woman in peace for a moment, do. Here's bread and meat for you, miss. Try to eat slowly, now, or you'll make yourself sick, for I doubt it's a long time since your last meal.'

When they had eaten their fill, Amabel jumped up again. 'And now we must see about a place for you to sleep. Meg, don't you think perhaps the guest room . . .?'

'No I do not, ma'am!' Meg said quickly, throwing her mistress a warning sideways glance. 'Whatever would the master say, if he knew you was asking in strangers, and not knowing anything about them?'

Amabel seemed little cowed at the prospect of her husband's disapproval, and jutted out her lip defiantly. 'But we do know about them, Meg, and look how tired they are, poor things. We can't turn them out, for I'm sure they have nowhere to sleep.'

Eugenie roused herself to make an effort, and standing up, she said, 'I do not wish in the least to be a trouble to you, madame, but if you have some outhouse, perhaps, or barn, for we have never been accustomed to sleep in the open, and I'm afraid – ' She glanced at Marie, but was herself swaying with weariness.

'There, you see, Meg, that proves they are respectable,' Amabel said anxiously. Meg folded her lips.

'Very well, ma'am, if you insist, they shall stay – but not the guest room. Why, they wouldn't expect it themselves, not the way they are. A mattress in the dairy will do them very well, I'm sure, and that's my last word on it.'

'Oh, very well,' Amabel said, disappointed. 'But try to make them comfortable, Meg, for I'm sure,' she added piously, 'the rector would say we ought to help anyone in such trouble. I'll go and see after some blankets.'

When she had gone, Eugenie turned her head to meet a long considering glance from Meg. 'Your mistress has a very kind heart,' she said.

'A great deal too kind,' Meg said tersely. 'She's no more sense than a kitten.'

'She is very fortunate to have such a faithful servant to take care of her,' Eugenie said.

'Aye, well,' Meg conceded, a little mollified. 'You were a gentlewoman in your own country, I suppose?'

'Yes,' said Eugenie.

Meg nodded. 'I thought so, from the way you ate. And there's something in the way you speak, too.' She nodded towards Marie, who was sitting on a stool at the table, drooping with weariness. 'She's your maid?'

'Yes.'

'Were you rich?'

Eugenie smiled. 'Yes, very.'

'Aye, well. Misfortune may come to anyone. You'll find things different now, I warrant.'

'We are told that God sees even the sparrow fall,' Eugenie said.

Meg looked surprised but gratified. 'Oh, so you read the Bible over there, do you? Well, that's as may be, but I've always found that God's a good deal too busy watching sparrows to concern Himself over the fate of us women. We've to take care of ourselves, and the sooner you learn that the better for you. Now we'd better get out the mattress, and see about filling it. There's plenty of clean straw in the shed at the back.' She glanced at Marie. '*She'll* not be much use to us. Can you bear to get your hands dirty, miss? Very well, come with me, then.'

'What is your master like?' Eugenie asked her a little later, as they thrust handfuls of straw into the canvas bag of the mattress. Meg's face gave away nothing, which Eugenie interpreted as disapproval.

'He's a fair master. Devoted to my mistress, though he might be a bit sharp with her from time to time.'

'Will he be angry with her for allowing us to stay?' Eugenie asked. 'I should not like to be the cause of trouble. We could be up and gone early in the morning, if need be.'

Meg regarded her with more approval than hitherto. 'Nay,' she said roughly, 'she'll twist him about her finger, never fear. I see now you're a proper, decent sort, and I'll tell him so. I'd have let you have the guest room,' she added almost placatingly, 'but you're that dirty, miss, it must be said, and I didn't know – '

'You were quite in the right,' Eugenie said soothingly. 'After the place we stayed in last night, we may very well have fleas. How I long for a bath!'

'A bath!' Meg was startled. 'Don't say you have baths over there too? Why, I never did!'

'Oh yes,' Eugenie said, laughing. 'We are not, perhaps, so very different from you, Meg.'

'You shall have hot water in the morning,' Meg promised stoutly, 'before Master gets home. Both of you!'

Meg was as good as her promise, and both women had bathed in front of the kitchen fire in as much hot water as they could wish, and dressed again, before the young mistress of the house was astir. Eugenie and Marie put on the clean linen from their cloak bag – Meg eyed it interestedly as it emerged and sucked her teeth over the fineness of the linen and the abundance of the lace – and then Meg produced an old dress of her own for Marie, and a plain lilac cambric gown of her mistress's for Eugenie. Marie dressed Eugenie's hair under Meg's watchful eye, who said when it was done, 'Well, if you don't look a proper lady after all, and a great deal better in that gown than ever Miss Amabel did!'

Eugenie was worried about Marie, who seemed flushed and low and out of sorts. 'I am sure you are beginning a cold,' she said, hanging over her solicitously. Marie, who was also sure she was, dismissed the idea with an attempt at briskness.

'It is nothing, mademoiselle, truly. I am very strong.' She could not afford, she reflected, to be ill, for the likelihood was that they would have to set off again as soon as the master came home, and continue their interrupted walk to London.

The daily servants appeared, and stared with their mouths open at the two strangers until Meg grew exasperated and drove them off to their tasks. To remove herself from her mistress's anxious eye, Marie took the bucket of hen food from Meg's hand and went off to feed them for her, and Eugenie, seeing there was nothing she could do to help Meg, who was preparing her mistress's tray, found herself a bowl and drew off some water, and prepared to wash out the underlinen she and Marie had been wearing. Meg paused for a moment to watch her, and then with a satisfied nod picked up the tray and left her alone.

The master arrived home shortly afterwards, when the young mistress was still sitting up in bed in a froth of lace and ribbons, sipping her chocolate and chattering to Meg, who was tidying the room and laying out Amabel's clothes and listening with only half an ear. At the sound of the horses' hooves she rushed to the window in time to see Mr McKendrick and his manservant disappearing round the back of the house.

'There now, and if I don't hurry up and get downstairs, he'll walk right in on that Frenchwoman washing her things, for you know he always comes in by the kitchen when he's in his riding boots.'

Amabel clasped her hands together in rapture, and almost spilled her chocolate. 'Goodness, yes; I had quite forgot! Don't let him be cross with them, dearest Meg! In fact, I think you had better send him directly up to me, so that I can explain it all to him. Dearest James! How glad I shall be to see him. Wait – before you go, please do give me the hand mirror, and my hairbrush. I'm sure I must look a perfect fright. Shall I just thread a ribbon through my hair, do you think?'

By the time Meg managed to get away, it was already too late. James McKendrick, having been thoroughly startled by the sight of a strange woman feeding his hens and calling to them in what was indisputably a foreign language, strode into the kitchen to demand an explanation of Meg, only to find another strange woman washing underlinen and singing a song under her breath in what sounded suspiciously like French!

James KcKendrick was a tall, good-looking young man in whom a tendency to think well of himself had suffered no setback from the circumstance of his early preferment in his chosen profession. He was blond, blue-eyed and fair-skinned, with a tendency to blush easily when vexed, and finely chiselled features which did not lend themselves readily to laughter. He was very fond of his wife, and thought her, on the whole rightly, a foolish creature who

28

needed to be looked after. He was a fair master, and a good husband, if one could set aside a liking always to be right, and a certain closeness with money. When he entered the kitchen his blue eyes were hot, his cheeks red, and his nostrils flaring, and he faced Eugenie with a look of righteous indignation. James McKendrick did not like to be startled in his own back yard, and still less in his own kitchen. Eugenie hastily withdrew her hands from the water and reached for a towel. With one comprehensive glance she summed him up as costive, and everyone knew that constipated men were worst tempered in the morning.

'What the devil is going on? Who the devil are you? Where's Meg? Damn it, can't a man leave his home for one day without everything going to the deuce? Meg! Amabel! And who is that woman out there laying spells on my hens like a damn witch?'

'She is my maid, Marie,' Eugenie said pleasantly. 'I beg your pardon, monsieur, if you were startled. It was unfortunate.'

The blood was receding from his cheeks a little. Those young men who had been badly in love with Eugenie at the time of her coming out had often said that her voice was one of her best features, and that she could have charmed Saint Paul himself with it. 'And who are you, ma'am, if I may ask?' he growled with a little more restraint.

'I am Eugenie Marie Christine Hélène d'Issy-Sable, Comtesse de Talcy,' said Eugenie, who knew a snob when she saw one. 'I have escaped from the revolutionary government in Paris and I seek refuge in England. I arrived at your house last night, in grave need of food and shelter, and your wife was gracious enough to offer them. She is,' she added, watching him narrowly, 'most completely a gentlewoman.'

Only the flaring nostrils now betrayed McKendrick's inner turmoil. His Grecian features were once more marble-smooth and pale, and Eugenie, noting the slightest tendency of his eyes to pop, was satisfied that her

29

alimentary diagnosis was correct. Blackberry leaf tea, she told herself, or chopped horehound leaves sprinkled on his food. Hadn't Amabel's mother taught her anything in those six months before her wedding?

'Wait here,' was all he said now, and he strode vigorously through the door which led to the rest of the house. Eugenie went peaceably back to her washing, and listened to the muted sounds of explosion, explanation and exhortation from above. It was, she conceded, quite a large story to swallow first thing in the morning, when a man had not even communed successfully with nature yet. She had wrung out and hung out the linen, and was engaged in brushing the now dry mud from her black gown, when Meg came back into the kitchen with the empty tray.

'Master wants to see you,' she said tersely, rolling her eyes expressively upwards. 'I meant to be back down before he arrived, but there! Anyway, Miss Amabel's smoothed his feathers, bless her, so don't go stirring him up again, and you'll be all right. In the parlour – through there, and the second door on the left.'

When Eugenie entered the parlour, she saw the master sitting very upright in a chair by the fireplace, while his wife, dressed in exactly the wrong shade of green, with a blue ribbon threading her curls, hung over him, engaged, it seemed, in kissing the top of his head and pulling the lobe of his ear with eager affection. He shrugged her off abruptly as Eugenie came in, and a spot of vexation appeared on each cheek. 'Ah, mademoiselle! Amabel, restrain yourself, my dear.'

But Amabel could hardly have heard the rebuke, for she had already straightened up, clasped her hands and cried, 'Oh, here she is! And how pretty you look, Eugenie, so much better than in that dreadful old black thing. That is my lilac cambric, is it not? I'm glad Meg gave it to you, for I never liked it, and it suits you very well, does it not, James? Oh, by the by, this is my husband, Mr James McKendrick, whom I spoke of yesterday. And this is Eugenie, James dear, but I can't remember the rest of her names. How prettily you have dressed your hair, Eugenie! I wish I had half your skill! How is your friend this morning?'

'Marie is a little unwell, I fear,' Eugenie began, but was interrupted by the master of the house, who looked sternly at his wife.

'That is not her friend, Bel, it is her maid. How you do run on! Please let me speak to mademoiselle without interruption.'

Amabel seemed impervious to rebuke. She smiled airily at him and said without rancour, 'Oh, I can see I shall only make you cross if I stay! I shall go down to the kitchen and talk to Meg about dinner, and see for myself how Marie fares. I wish she may not take a fever – you were both so very damp when you arrived last night! Perhaps Meg should make her up a draught, for you know we have no physician nearer than Kingston, and he is so very old I'm sure he doesn't know what he is about. When I lived at home with Mama and Papa, we had two physicians and an apothecary, all within a few streets of us. But that was at Tunbridge, which was a much larger place than Kingston, and our house was right in the middle of the town, you know, which was very convenient for shopping, though Papa used to say that the noise of carriages passing the windows was beyond anything. But only see James glare at me! He says I am such a chatterbox, it is quite shocking!' And she dimpled irrepressibly at them both, and tripped away, leaving Eugenie at the mercy of her husband.

When they were alone, McKendrick half rose from his chair and gestured Eugenie towards the sofa. 'Won't you sit down, mademoiselle?' He watched critically as Eugenie crossed the room and sat gracefully, folding her slender hands in her lap. 'I should be obliged,' he continued, 'if you would tell me your history. My wife is anxious that I should be of assistance to you, and to be so I must know a little more of your circumstances.'

Eugenie obliged, telling him briefly who she was and

how and why she came to arrive penniless at his door the night before. He listened attentively, a frown between his brows, his fingertips placed judicially together, and when she had finished he put one or two questions to her, very much, she thought, as though he were cross-examining a witness.

'So, mademoiselle, you place your hopes on the arrival of your servants with your jewels?'

'I do not depend upon it,' Eugenie answered evenly. 'If they were prevented from reaching St Omer, it is likely that they were taken into custody, and the jewels confiscated. But I must go to Brompton and make enquiries, for that is where they will go, if they do escape from France.'

'And if they do not reach England, what then? You have no friends or relatives in England, I collect?'

'No relatives, monsieur. Of friends, I hope to find many in London.'

'Emigrants like yourself?'

'Assuredly.'

'And how, if I may ask, do you propose to support yourself and your maid?'

Eugenie shrugged. 'Marie and I must find work. Perhaps I may be a governess. I can teach music, dancing, drawing, the French language. Or perhaps I may be a dressmaker. Marie and I are both skilled with the needle.'

McKendrick nodded coolly. 'To sum up, you mean to walk to London, entrust your immediate welfare to other emigrants you hope to meet there, and seek employment. You, who until now have lived in a palace, commanded servants, and never worked for your living.'

Eugenie looked down at her hands. 'One must do what is necessary,' she said in a subdued voice.

McKendrick stood up, clasped his hands behind his back, and walked about the room a little in thought. Then he came back to stand before her. 'Mademoiselle,' he said, 'I have a proposition to put before you. My wife, as you see, is very young, and not very wise in the ways of the world.

I am a great deal from home in the course of my work, and this leaves her alone, except for Meg. I had cause to dismiss her maid, and though Meg is devoted to her, she has too much to do about the house to be happy escorting Bel when she goes out, and it would not be suitable for her to go out unaccompanied.' Eugenie nodded assent. 'Now you seem to me to be a woman of refinement and sense. I propose that you remain here for a period, and act as companion and mentor to my wife: take her about, advise her in her duties, polish her a little.' Eugenie began to speak, but he raised his hand. 'No, hear me out. In return, I will furnish you with clothing and pay you a wage, so that when you go to London, you will have a cushion against the harshness of a world I am persuaded you know nothing about.'

'But I must make enquiries about my other servants,' Eugenie said.

'I understand that; but assure yourself, ma'am, that I can make such enquiries on your behalf a great deal more efficiently than you. I go to London regularly upon business, and have clerks who are frequently employed in the task of seeking information, and may be supposed to have some skill in the matter. Reflect: you are a female, alone and without resources.'

Eugenie reflected. There was a great deal of truth in what he said, and she had secretly been dreading a continuation of the humiliating destitution of which she had had a brief taste. She had no idea of how to go about making enquiries after Pierre and Nana, or how to find lodgings or employment if it proved necessary. A man's help in all this would be welcome. Besides, she liked what she had seen of the young Mrs McKendrick, and longed to do something to right the maddening wrongness of her clothing and *toilette*. Besides again, she was convinced Marie was beginning a feverish cold, and ought not to travel further.

'What of Marie?' she asked.

McKendrick nodded. 'Your maid may attend you and

Mrs McKendrick, and make herself useful about the house. I will pay her a wage too. She can share a room with Meg. You, I propose, should have the guest room, as befits your rank.'

Eugenie rose. 'Then, monsieur, I accept with gratitude. You will make my enquiries for me, and I will act as your wife's companion – for a short while.'

She offered her hand, and McKendrick took it, and unexpectedly, for the first time, he smiled. The difference was devastating.

Chapter Three

'There now, what do you think?' said Eugenie, carefully removing the pins from her mouth. Amabel turned around to survey her image in the looking glass. It was a full-length cheval glass: nothing that money alone could achieve was lacking in this house.

'Oh, indeed it's lovely! Quite, quite beautiful!' Amabel cried gratifyingly, pressing her clasped hands to her bosom, and then flinging them wide the better to see the line of the dress Eugenie and Marie had fashioned for her. It was made of a fine sarsenet of a delicate shade of pale, soft yellow – if the colour of buttercups were a liquid like milk, this silk was the colour of the cream it would put up. It had a low-cut, tight-fitting bodice, with the raised waistline which was now being seen everywhere. The skirt fell straight in front just to the ground, and at the back was fuller, gathered over a false-rump, and extending gracefully behind in a short train. The sleeves were short for evening wear and quite plain, with a small cuff, a keyhole fastening and two pearl buttons. There was a row of the same buttons on the bodice, where the two halves joined at the front, and these, with the double row of braided satin ribbon trimming the hem, were the only decoration.

'I had not thought anything so plain could be so becoming,' Amabel said naively, twisting her neck to look at the back of the gown. 'Only look how it falls at the back! I wonder that Mrs Sedgeley could never make my gowns to fall like that!'

'Too little cloth,' Marie said tersely. She had seen enough examples of that mantuamaker's art to have formed a very low opinion of her.

Amabel opened her eyes wide. 'Oh no, I'm sure it could not be that, for I always bought plenty. My blue muslin, you know, took a full ten yards in the making, for I saw the bill from Layton's on Mr McKendrick's writing desk. Ten yards of *bleu celeste* mull muslin at seven and sevenpence the yard, sent direct to Mrs Sedgeley's, and even with the flounces, there must have been nine yards good for the gown itself.'

'Zere is not nine yards in zat gown,' said Marie firmly, and catching her mistress's eye, added in French, 'I wonder how many ladies in Kingston bought blue muslin aprons, very cheap, from this Madame Sedgeley? If there is seven yards in that horrible gown it is more than I would vouch for.'

'Well, there was nothing left over, for I asked Mrs Sedgeley if there was enough to get out a kerchief to match,' said Amabel, undisturbed, 'and she said it was all used up. But I do love this gown, Eugenie. How clever you are! Do all French ladies make their own gowns? But are you sure it isn't too plain for an evening party? You don't think it wants a flounce or two, or a bit of lace somewhere? I should hate anyone to think that Mr McKendrick cannot afford the best.'

'It wants nothing,' said Eugenie firmly. 'Fineness of dress should lie in having the best materials and the smallest stitches, that's all. Your friends will think you very handsome, I promise you, and look at their own gowns with dissatisfaction.'

That was what Amabel wanted to hear. 'I think they must,' she said with a happy sigh, her eyes on her image in the glass. The creamy colour complemented her fine skin and golden curls, without quarrelling with her eyes, and the simplicity of the style only drew attention to her prettiness. 'And I have my long French kid gloves, which are nicer than anything I have seen in Kingston. But what necklace must I wear? I wish I had diamonds. Mrs Henry Baker has a diamond necklet with fourteen stones in it, and earrings to match – though to be sure, they were her mother's, and the setting is very old and not at all pretty.'

Eugenie thought painfully of her own jewels, now no doubt adorning the unworthy body of some revolutionary minister's wife. She thought of the diamond tiara, with a hundred and ten stones of different sizes set into a lacework of flowers, which she had worn at the dress ball at Versailles. Her court gown had been of cream and shell-pink striped silk brocade, and she had danced with the young Duc de Veslne in the Galerie des Glaces, where a thousand candles had flung their light into the magnificent long mirrors, and the crystal drops hanging from the gilded sconces and chandeliers had split it into rainbow dazzle all around them.

With an inward sigh she dragged herself back to the contemplation of Amabel's envy of Mrs Henry Baker. She had heard a great deal about this young woman during the weeks she had been Amabel's companion and mentor, and had gathered that she was a year or two older than Amabel, married to a prosperous tradesman who, having made his fortune in the china business, had retired from it determined to achieve gentility for himself and his descendants. He had married a Miss Camberley, daughter of a country physician, with three thousand pounds, though the dowry was unimportant to him, compared with the fact that she was untainted by any connection with trade: her grandfather had been a clergyman, her great-grandfather a freeholder. Amabel felt that Mrs Henry Baker put on unwarranted airs, considering the land-owning great-grandfather had been, in truth, little better than a grazier, and a physician was far below a fully fledged lawyer on the social scale. Mr Henry Baker, moreover, was not genteel, and though the former Miss Camberley might now command an allowance more than double Amabel's own, her dowry had been paltry compared with Amabel's ten thousand pounds.

Marie, whose English was improving rapidly, heard the story from Meg in the kitchen, and though Meg was righteously indignant on her nurseling's behalf, Marie could only curl her lip at the thought of her mistress's being subjected to the whims of this little *bourgeoise* whose sole ambition was to outdress the daughter of a country doctor. Eugenie, who was as beautiful as a star, and whose every drop of blood was a hundred times more noble than that of the King of England himself, had, however, the patience and sweet temper of an angel, and had entered herself completely, to Marie's regret, into the concerns of this wretched little household; and where she led, Marie could only follow. An evening party was to be held, an elaborate affair with music, cards and supper, and as it would be Mrs James McKendrick's first formal entertainment, she wanted very badly to shine.

It would not be Eugenie's fault if she did not. Everything, from the issuing of the invitations down to the composition of the supper had gone under her scrutiny, and the affair was to be as elegant as she could contrive. Mr McKendrick's unfortunate disinclination to part from his money had been temporarily overcome by his consciousness of Eugenie's rank, intellect and education. A combined fear of appearing foolish and a desire to look well in her eyes prevented him from demurring at the expense of anything she suggested. It was fortunate that he liked good food and fine wines, for she was able to enlist his enthusiasm over the supper menu, and with the subtle and manipulative skill she had learned from her father she had persuaded him that an open-handedness in regard to the quantity of the refreshment provided could only draw attention to its superb quality, and raise him immeasurably in the esteem of his guests.

He had been grateful when Eugenie offered to make his wife's gown for the occasion with her own hands and Marie's help. It had been necessary, since Amabel had no dressmaking skills of her own, to have her gowns made up professionally, and since Mrs Sedgeley was the most fashionable mantuamaker in Kingston, Amabel could not well be seen to patronise anyone else. His parsimony would not allow of purchasing her gowns in London, since he was sure they would charge twice or three times the money for the same amount of work, which offended his sensibilities; but he had not been entirely convinced of Mrs Sedgeley's honesty, nor completely happy with the results.

He had no natural refinement of taste, and was unable to say why Amabel's gowns would not do, but in the course of his profession he entered many a society man's drawing room, and he was aware that his wife did not look quite like theirs. Soon after their arrival, Eugenie and Marie had made over Amabel's lilac cambric gown for Eugenie's use, altering the cut and sewing on a trimming of black ribbon, since Eugenie was still in mourning. The difference they had made to the gown had convinced McKendrick that they knew what Mrs Sedgeley did not.

Eugenie had enjoyed shopping with Amabel, though she was surprised that the young woman should be contented with the limited facilities offered by Kingston; but Layton's, the leading linen draper, was a fine shop with an excellent range of cloth, and here Eugenie had been able to steer Amabel away from the violent blues and greens she so loved. McKendrick, in recognition that there would be no making up to pay for, had told Eugenie that she might buy lengths for two new gowns for herself, so her pleasure in examining the bales and fingering the cambrics, muslins, silks and crapes had not been entirely altruistic. The formidable Mr Layton himself, learning of the presence in his shop of a Frenchwoman who understood cloth, came out from his lair, bowed to the ladies, and offered them his personal assistance. In a short time he was deep in a comfortable conversation with Eugenie, to whom he accorded the supreme accolade of treating her as an equal. Amabel, who had seen even such stately personages as Mrs Holland Burrage shrivelled by Layton's steely eye and exquisitely courteous contempt, could only gaze, wide-eyed and almost open-mouthed, as he chuckled at something Eugenie had said and asked her cordially for her opinion of a bale of French silk gauze he had come by. He even brought out from its hiding place some exquisite Valenciennes lace which he said, with a wistful look, he had been saving for the right lady.

He applauded Eugenie's choice for Amabel of the pale yellow sarsenet, the shade of which, he told Eugenie to her barely concealed amusement, was called *soupir du papillon*. It said a great deal for Amabel's good nature that she did not object when Layton spent as much time and trouble over the choice of material for Eugenie's gown for the evening party, or when he guided her away from a modest violet poplin and towards a superb dove-coloured silk crape, whose matte surface, he said, with an eye on Eugenie's black ribbons, would be quite suitable for half-mourning. Eugenie shook her head doubtfully, with a glance at Amabel. But she smiled and pressed Eugenie's arm and said, 'Oh do take the crape! It is far and away the nicer, and I want you to appear to advantage before my friends. You must not regard the expense – *I* do not, I assure you!' Whether Mr McKendrick would object or not was another matter, Eugenie thought, but allowed herself to be persuaded.

On the evening of the party, she and Marie helped Amabel to dress. Marie resented the fact that Amabel saw nothing incongruous in having Eugenie act as her abigail, and firmly twitched each garment out of Eugenie's hands as she took them up, reducing her part in the business to that of supervision. On went the chemise, the stays, the pocket, the false-rump, the long silk stockings and the garters, while Amabel stood rigid with excitement, almost holding her breath, to the detriment of her pearly complexion. Finally, allowing Eugenie to take a hand, Marie lifted on the dress and settled it.

Eugenie had persuaded Amabel that nothing would more become her than pearls. 'Only a very young woman can wear them to effect,' she lied nobly, 'for it needs a perfect skin and a fair complexion to show them off properly.'

'Mrs Henry Baker is very dark-skinned,' Amabel mused, going to the heart of the matter. 'And to be sure, she must be nearly five and twenty by now. I'm sure you're right. Pearls it should be.'

She had two ropes of pearls, a short one which had been her wedding present from her husband, and a long rope of inferior pearls which her father had given her at her coming out. Eugenie persuaded her to wear the shorter string around her throat.

'And the long string I think you should wear in your hair, for they will look very pretty, and no one else will have a headdress like it. Everyone else, I dare say, will be wearing feathers, so yours will be out of the common.'

This idea took at once, and when she was dressed, Amabel sat down before her dressing table while Marie cut and dressed her hair, and then Eugenie contrived a very pretty effect with the pearls and some knots of white satin ribbon. When Amabel at last pronounced herself satisfied, Marie was able to hurry her mistress away and dress her before going down to the kitchen to help Meg with the last preparations for supper.

Eugenie's gown of dove-coloured silk was plainer even than Amabel's, but very becoming, with a crossover bodice and a short train. The sleeves were pretty, with an inverse pleat and a long cuff edged with a band of black ribbon, but as Marie dressed her hair, Eugenie mourned the lack of any jewellery to complete her *toilette*. She thought of her pearls – finer by far than Amabel's – left behind in Chichester, and irredeemable unless McKendrick should pay her wages far in excess of anything she expected.

When she had thanked Marie and sent her away, she sat for a while at the window of the little guest chamber and considered her lot. She had been lucky, she knew, to find such kindness as was shown to her here at Ivy Cottage, and she did not often allow herself the luxury of repining; but there was no denying that she was restless and unhappy, grieving for Papa and for her homeland, worried about the future, and exceedingly bored. It was not in her nature to sulk, and she had flung herself wholeheartedly into the concerns of the household and its mistress; but she had too little to do, nothing that challenged her intellect, no companion with whom she could converse on equal terms. Amabel was an amiable fool: kind, innocuously vain, but stupid. Her husband was clever in his way, but blinkered by selfishness, ambition, and snobbery.

He had kept his promise to carry out enquiries on her behalf, but there had been no news of Pierre or Nana. No one amongst the emigrant population in Brompton had heard of them, and even a reward offered for information had yielded nothing. McKendrick also made enquiries about the *Hirondelle*, the boat Eugenie had hoped to take from St Omer, and a man had come forward who claimed to have been on it. As far as his story could be checked, he seemed to be telling the truth. The *Hirondelle* had set sail before the storm had begun, intending to land the passengers and a cargo of smuggled brandy on a deserted beach on Romney Marsh, in Kent.

As they neared the shore, however, the alarm had been given that the customs men were out. The boat had put about and proceeded, at a safe distance from the shore, up the coast to make a landfall near Southend at the mouth of the Thames, where the passengers were put down. Intending then to return to Romney Marsh with the brandy, the *Hirondelle* had been caught in the storm which had driven Eugenie down the Channel, and, unable to make enough sea room for herself, she had been driven ashore near Rochester. The informant, who had been one of the crew, has escaped apprehension by the customs authorities and had hidden out amongst the *émigré* population, trying to earn enough money to make his way back to France. McKendrick's reward for information about the *Hirondelle* brought him nervously out of hiding, but all he could tell them was that no one answering the description of Pierre and Nana had come on board the ship at St Omer.

It seemed certain, therefore, that they had been taken by the gendarmes in Abbeville, and if that were so, the d'Issy jewels would now be part of the revolutionary government's treasure. This meant, as far as Eugenie was concerned, that she must find some way to earn her living, and that she would have to do so for the rest of her life. It was a frightening thought. She was strong, healthy, intelligent, and energetic; but she was gently born, and had never in her life contemplated taking up responsibility for herself. There had always been Papa, and a house full of servants, and money, and the future she had always expected was of eventual marriage to some wealthy and nobly born man, of becoming mistress of a large household and mother to a large family. The day-to-day problems of finding food to put in her mouth and a place to lay her head at night had not been part of the picture, and contemplating them now made her heart fail and her courage waver. She had no idea how one went about it. Better, in that case, to remain at Ivy Cottage: whatever the tedium, whatever the humiliation, it must be worse to starve to death in the gutter.

She sighed, and then shook herself and smiled ruefully. Here she was in a new gown of beautiful silk crape about to go down to an elegant supper in a warm and comfortable house, and all she could think about was how much she had lost! She got up from the window seat and knelt.

Crossing herself, she prayed briefly but vehemently to be saved from the sins of pride and ingratitude, and then rose and went downstairs with a light tread.

The guests arrived. The dread Mrs Henry Baker revealed herself as a swart brunette in puce satin trimmed with a good deal of lace, and a head-dress of tall plumes. The Camberley diamonds were much in evidence, Mrs Henry Baker frequently drawing attention to them by her habit of putting her gloved hand to her bosom and sighing, so that the heaving of her chest made them catch the light. She had a loud voice and effusive manners, and altogether was exactly the kind of vulgar, underbred, overdressed young woman that Eugenie had been expecting to see. There was no doubt, however, that she drew attention to herself, and as she surged across the drawing room towards her hostess, with her hands outstretched and her tall plumes waving perilously close to the candles in the chandelier, her effusive words of greeting bubbling over like lava, Amabel cast a doubtful glance towards Eugenie as if to seek assurance that she had not modelled herself upon the wrong pattern.

'Dearest Amabel, my sweet, how wonderful to see you! I have not spoken to you this age! What have you been doing with yourself, you dear creature?' Her greedy eye flicked over the hair, pearls, and gown. 'But where did you get such a delicious gown? Don't tell me you got it from London? Oh yes, I know, I can tell at a glance! Believe me, it says London in every line, positively cries out London! And what a cunning way you have dressed your head! Is it your own thought? You sly thing, you mean to shine us all down!'

Mr Henry Baker, a step behind her, kept his silence: a stout, hale, elderly man with a port-drinker's nose, and an ingratiating smile fixed permanently on his face. He was content to let his wife lead the way, regarding her with a half-astonished admiration, as if he could not believe

44

his own good fortune in catching her. He was wearing green satin small-clothes with white silk stockings and a bottle-green velvet coat, while his waistcoat was a triumph of green, gold and purple shot silk, irridescent as a pigeon's neck in the candlelight. Eugenie tore her gaze from it with difficulty, and Mr Baker, tearing his from his wife's plumes, caught her eye and gave her a conspiratorial wink. She had no idea what he meant by it, but as the evening progressed, she found the gesture repeated whenever she happened to look at him. Since he did not speak a word the whole evening, she formed the impression that the wink was his only means of communication and took to responding with a slight bow of the head, which seemed to please him.

The next guests to arrive were McKendrick's principal, Mr Spennilow, and his wife, dignified elderly people, slow speaking and self-important. The rest of the company was made up of young men of the legal profession, McKendrick's friends and their wives, some neighbours, and the wealthy residents of Kingston who were McKendrick's principal clients. There was no doubt that in her new style, Amabel stood out from the company in glowing contrast, and Eugenie saw many covert and puzzled glances directed towards her as the other young ladies tried to discover what it was about dear Amabel's gown that was so special.

Eugenie herself was introduced very kindly to the company, and was received by the young people with curiosity and enthusiasm, and by the older folk with indifference or faint disapproval. The young legal gentlemen were eager for first-hand news about events in Paris, and she was soon the centre of a rapt group who flung questions at her and listened with flattering attention to all she had to say. This made Amabel very proud; Mrs Henry Baker, who was used to being the centre of attention herself, very cross; and McKendrick, who thought something improper might be about to happen in his drawing room, a little nervous.

He was glad when the last guest arrived, very late, as was her custom, making an entrance which Mrs Henry Baker would have been glad to emulate, and drawing all attention, however unwillingly, to herself.

It was none other than the formidable Mrs Holland Burrage, Kingston's richest widow and, in her own eyes at least, the leader of its society. She combined the advantage of being a large woman with a predilection for purple silk. Her head was swathed in a gold-cloth turban decorated with purple feathers and gold tassels; her large-featured face seemed designed for expressing hauteur; and her important bosom for the better display of a spreading necklace of diamonds large enough to make the former Miss Camberley's look like dust-motes. As she sailed in, all conversation faltered and failed: all eyes were fixed on her, and hers swept the room so regally that Eugenie half-expected the women to sink in curtsies as they did at Versailles when the Queen passed.

McKendrick, raising himself a few points in Eugenie's estimation, went forward to greet her without obvious obsequiousness, deftly brought Mr and Mrs Spennilow into the circle, and established a conversation amongst them. It was nicely done, she acknowledged. Tentatively, other conversations started up, and finding they were not rebuked, rapidly gained confidence.

'This lady, who is she?' Eugenie enquired of the nearest young legal gentleman, whose name was Martin. He was unmarried. His clothes were shiny at elbow and knee, and there seemed to be a trace of brown sauce on his waistcoat, and more than a trace of ink on his fingers; but Eugenie liked him. He seemed intelligent, and more independent in his opinions than the rest of the company, and she had caught him regarding Mrs Henry Baker's puce satin with a very satirical eye.

'Widow of Holland Burrage, the wine merchant,' he replied succinctly. '*Her* family were brewers, rich as Croesus. She had twenty thousand pounds when she married Burrage, and that was in those days.' He nodded significantly. 'She had the *in* in London, or so she says, and knew everyone, all the *ton*. But she retired to Kingston when Burrage died, and she's been queening it over us ever since.' He nodded his head towards McKendrick, who was standing at the dowager's elbow, inclining his handsome head towards her moving mouth. 'McKendrick hopes to get her business, of course. Flying high! He toad-eats her shamelessly, but he's a good lawyer, and she's a shrewd old creature, for all her ways, so they may yet deal together. Spennilow would be in ecstasies if McKendrick landed her! He plays her cleverly, but she ain't in the net yet, not by a long stretch. She'll have her game of him, before she rolls over; for it's my belief she's half in love with him, you know. He's a handsome enough devil, if you like white marble. I've always thought him a cold fish, but perhaps like calls to like.'

Eugenie listened in perplexity to all this, for she had thought she spoke English rather well, but a good deal of what Martin said had been incomprehensible. 'I see,' she said. He smiled at her.

'Is it you that's responsible for Mrs McKendrick's new style? Yes, I thought so. I don't know much about females and fashion, but one look at you says it all. Mrs McK. looks a different creature. She always was pretty, but now she might pass anywhere, as long as she don't open her mouth. I wish McKendrick may not regret it! He has ambitions to set up in London, and if he takes Mrs McK. there looking as she does, he will find out all he needs to know about society's little ways. But he may not have been a bad friend to you, mamzelle, after all – see, Mrs Holland Burrage is looking at you. Trust her to know how the milk got into the coconut!'

'Why should I want this lady to look at me?' Eugenie asked with raised brows.

'Now don't give me that frosty look,' he said with an impish grin. 'It don't need a genius to know that you're in trouble, or a lady of your quality wouldn't be staying here with the McKendricks at all. Mrs B. may be a prosy old bore, but she's horrid rich, and as shrewd as she can hold together. If she decided to help you, you'd be helped, sure as a gun. God,' he added fervently, 'I wish she'd decide to take *me* under her wing!'

It was not long afterwards that Eugenie found McKendrick at her elbow. 'Mrs Holland Burrage would like to meet you,' he told her impressively, and stood back a step the better to survey her face.

'Really?' she managed to say.

McKendrick nodded and began to guide her through the throng. 'You caught her eye, and she told me I might present you to her.'

Eugenie conjured up a brief but gratifying picture of Mrs Holland Burrage at Versailles asking to be introduced to the Comtesse de Talcy, and, thus fortified, went meekly to her fate.

It was not quite as bad as she had expected. Once she had got past the purple silk and flashing diamonds, she found a shrewd and not unintelligent eye in the dowager's high-nosed face, and the harsh voice which questioned her, though peremptory, needed to ask nothing twice. Mrs Holland Burrage dismissed McKendrick with a wave of the hand and settled down to extract Eugenie's whole history, a process which took little more than a quarter of an hour. At the end of that time, Eugenie found she had told the story of her flight and a great deal about her family and childhood. To do her justice, the widow did not allow herself to be influenced in any way by the discovery that Eugenie's father was an earl.

'Of course,' she said severely, 'that makes you a countess in your own right, the way you do things over there, but in this country we don't hold with it. In England, the children of the nobility are commoners. That makes the title worth having, you see,' she explained, not unkindly. 'Your way, earls and suchlike are two for a penny. Now if you were a countess in England . . .' She paused to let the golden vision hover before Eugenie's eyes a moment before dispelling it. 'However, there's no saying but what it could be of use to you. You have no English relatives, I suppose?'

'No, madame,' said Eugenie patiently.

'Nor friends of the family? Did your papa never come to England?'

'No, madame. My great-aunt was educated in England with an English family, but that was long ago, and – '

'What family was that, child?' Mrs Holland Burrage demanded.

'The Earl of St Osyth. My great-aunt was brought up with the daughter of the house for two years, but – '

'Her name? What was her name?'

'My aunt's name?'

'No, no, the name of the daughter of the house, of course.'

'It was the Lady Mary Freed,' Eugenie said, and was startled when the dowager clapped a hand like a side of meat on her shoulder.

'Well, child, why didn't you say so? What on earth are you doing here? Why didn't you go to her straight away? If she and your aunt were childhood friends, you cannot think that she would refuse to give you a home with her. The McKendricks are good people, certainly, but this is not the place for you, when you might do better.'

Eugenie delicately shifted out from under the restraining hand. 'Madame, you do not understand. My great-aunt de Narrandais was very old. She is dead now, and the friend of her childhood is surely also dead. It was a very long time ago.'

'Don't talk to me in that foolish way,' Mrs Holland Burrage said sharply. 'Do you take me for a simpleton? Would I tell you to go and live with someone who was dead?'

'You mean – Lady Mary Freed is still alive?' Eugenie asked foolishly.

'Haven't I already said so?' snapped the dowager. 'She's Lady Mary Berrington now – married Sir Arthur Berrington, one of Pitt's cronies – but he's been dead these fifteen years. She lives in Brook Street. I used to see her for ever when I lived in London. At least, I met her once or twice, for she did not go about much, and she was always the highest of high-sticklers. She and Berrington never had any children of their own, so don't tell me she wouldn't welcome the child of her old schoolfriend.'

Eugenie was too stunned by this new turn of events to attempt to untangle the dowager's genealogical misapprehensions. Could it really be possible that Tante Alicie's dear friend was still alive? They had kept up a correspondence for years after the young Frenchwoman had returned to France, but it had ceased when the American wars broke out, and that was twenty years ago. Tante Alicie had always spoken of her friend as if she were dead, and Eugenie found it hard to adjust to the idea of her still existing, a real flesh-and-blood person. But even if she were alive, would she really, as Madame Burrage said, welcome Eugenie? Why, indeed, should she?

'But madame,' Eugenie managed to say at last, 'I do not know Lady Mary, and she does not know me. I cannot simply go to her house and say *me voici, madame*.'

'Of course not – who suggested you should?' Mrs Holland Burrage said, and her eyes took on a gleam. 'Haven't I told you I have the honour to be acquainted with Lady Mary? I shall be very happy to go and see her and explain the matter to her. McKendrick shall arrange it, and establish the bona fides. He can take up a letter from me. All these lawyers know one another, and if he does not know Lady Mary's man of business, I'll eat my hat – aye, feather and all. McKendrick! Come here, I have something particular to say to you.'

Now Eugenie understood that Mrs Holland Burrage's

eagerness in the matter was not simply a desire to be busy about other people's concerns, but to reintroduce herself into the circle of London society which, no doubt, she had sadly missed since her retirement to Kingston. McKendrick obeyed the summons and listened with his usual attention to what the widow had to say, but his eye, flickering to meet Eugenie's, conveyed to her the notion that he did not think the part Mrs Holland Burrage was sketching out for herself in the drama was either necessary or likely to advance their cause. The daughter of an earl, and a notable high-stickler, was not likely to welcome the intrusion into her circle of the socially ambitious daughter of a brewer; especially one with a predilection for purple satin.

Chapter Four

Mr James McKendrick found himself in a dilemma. He could not persuade himself that he was likely to arouse gratitude in Lady Mary Berrington by introducing Mrs Holland Burrage into her acquaintance and giving her an excuse to be calling whenever she had a mind; or that Lady Mary would be prompted to employ on any other business the man who performed his first task with so little address. On the other hand, the most delicate hint towards Mrs Holland Burrage that she might be excluded from the happy business of uniting Lady Mary with her childhood friend's great-niece had been received by the widow with cold-eyed hostility. His professional pride urged him to proceed with tact and delicacy and therefore without Mrs Holland Burrage; but at last self-interest reminded him that a rich brewer's daughter almost in the hand outweighed a baronet's widow who was certainly no closer than the bush, and that offending the queen of Kingston's society would put him in extremely bad odour with his principal, Mr Spennilow.

The business proceeded slowly, through introductory letters, and then a visit to Town by Mr McKendrick, for as Mrs Holland Burrage had rightly said, Lady Mary Berrington went out very little into society, and had many a faithful Cerberus with specific orders to prevent access to her. In the meantime, Eugenie's period of mourning had come to an end, and she was able to remove the black ribbons from her gowns; and Amabel had confided to her, rosy-cheeked and breathless, the news of her Expectations.

'Of course, it's too soon to be certain, but Meg says she is quite sure, and I must say that I think so too, because, you know,' with an ever deeper blush, 'nothing in the least like this has ever happened before. Oh Eugenie, I am so very happy! Nothing else was wanting to make me quite, quite happy, for of course James – Mr McKendrick – must want an heir, and Mama has written to me twice to ask whether I have anything to tell her, for you know she has been talking ever since I was fourteen and let down my skirts about being a grandmother and I should have *died* sooner than disappoint her! And now I shall want only to know that you are settled with Lady Mary to be the happiest creature alive!'

Eugenie thanked her for her good nature. 'But I'm afraid I have failed you badly, for I have not yet helped you to choose a suitable maid. If I go now to live with Lady Mary – though nothing is certain, of course – you will be without a companion.'

'Oh tush! Don't regard it,' said Amabel lightly. 'As to finding a maid, we can do that easily enough before you go. And of course Lady Mary will want you to go and live with her. She has no child or companion, and James says that *émigrés* are all the rage this year, and that every lady of the *ton* has a member of the French nobility to run tame about her house, and it will be worlds better for Lady Mary to have one who is almost a relative!'

Eugenie repressed a smile at this unflattering picture of her prospects. 'Then, ma'am, I must suppose that you will not miss me if I go.'

Amabel threw her arms about Eugenie affectionately. 'Oh, but I shall, quite dreadfully! For myself I wish you might stay here for ever, you dear creature, but James says that it will be better for you to go to London, and that there is no future for you here, and of course he is right.' She withdrew her embrace and sighed a little. 'With Lady Mary you will be able to go into society and make a splendid marriage, and then you will forget all about us. That's as it should be, of course, but I should have liked you to see my new baby, when he comes.'

'How can you think I would forget you, dear ma'am?' Eugenie said with gentle reproach. 'Am I so ungrateful? I can never forget all you have done for Marie and me, the kindness you showed us in taking us in. If Lady Mary does offer me a home – ' she hesitated ' – I cannot tell how I should be placed, and her wishes would have to be regarded, but you may be sure that I would write very often, and come to visit you whenever I could.'

Amabel smiled sunnily. 'Oh do not promise anything. Old ladies can be amazingly difficult, I know, and James says that Lady Mary is the stiffest of all. But now, what do you say to coming into Kingston with me? I must have a new hat for when James and I go to see Mama and Papa to tell them the News, and some new gloves, for my white ones are horrid soiled. And now that you are out of mourning, I think you ought to have a new gown – something smart for London, you know.'

'With pleasure,' Eugenie said. 'And while we are there, perhaps we ought to visit the exchange, to engage a maid for you?'

Amabel made a face. 'I suppose we must; but I don't want one like the last, a sour-faced thing who quarreled with Meg and made me feel foolish all the time.'

'It shall not be,' Eugenie said soothingly. 'She shall be just as you like.'

'Then she shall be just like you,' smiled Amabel, with a squeeze of Eugenie's arm.

The invitation which came at last from Lady Mary for Eugenie to come and see her was so cordially worded that Eugenie felt a rush of tears to her eyes. It was almost as if her dear aunt de Narrandais were still alive. She was to travel to Brook Street by post chaise, a luxury which her sojourn with the McKendricks had taught her to value at its true worth, although the knowledge that this luxury was owed to the fact that Mrs Holland Burrage was to accompany her, made her wish she might go up to Town on the back of a carrier's cart, as long as she could go alone.

'Four horses!' whispered Amabel, pinching Eugenie's arm as she stood in the doorway with her to say goodbye. 'James will be quite shocked. But Mrs Holland Burrage never spares expense. You will be in London before you can look about you.' She choked a little on the last words. Poor Amabel's face was swollen with tears, and she had hung so affectionately around Eugenie's neck that the collar of Eugenie's new pelisse was quite sodden.

Marie had already climbed into the chaise and taken the drop-seat, and Eugenie was waited for. Over Amabel's golden head she caught the eye of Dacres, the new maid, a smart and efficient woman in her late twenties, who had already endeared herself to Meg by sitting down on her first evening to swap confinements with her over the kitchen table. Dacres gave Eugenie a nod of complicity, and stepped forward to put a supporting and motherly arm around Amabel's waist so that Eugenie could detach herself and climb into the carriage. There was a flurry of waving, the postboys cracked their whips and the chaise jerked forward on its journey to London.

Eugenie would have been content merely to look out of the window at the passing countryside and marvel at how green and lush England was, and how very tidy! But the merest politeness demanded that she thank Mrs Holland Burrage for her kindness in conveying her to London, and the widow was not slow in seizing the opening.

'I am very glad to do so, my dear, for it gives me the opportunity to tell you a little about the ways of London society and prepare you for meeting Lady Mary. I should not like any little awkwardness on your part to spoil your chances with her, for you know first impressions are very important, and if she should happen to take a fancy to you, you would be established for ever.'

Eugenie could not quite leave this alone. In her gentlest manner she said, 'But my dear ma'am, I assure you I shall not be awkward. I am quite accustomed to going into company, you know. In Paris I was frequently acting as my father's hostess, since my mother died – '

'Exactly!' Mrs Holland Burrage exclaimed triumphantly. 'You have not had the benefit of a mother's guidance, my dear; and besides, London society is not at all like Paris society. We have a very different way of doing things from you French, take my word for it.'

Eugenie repressed the desire to enquire of Mrs Holland Burrage how much she knew of Paris society, or to point out that a young woman brought up to navigate the shoals of the tortuous etiquette of Versailles was hardly likely to go aground in a Brook Street drawing room. She set herself to listen quietly as Mrs Holland Burrage told her how to behave in the presence of an earl's daughter, and drew her amusement from observing the growing indignation on Marie's face as the widow went on to explain the mechanics of being presented to the Queen at one of the drawing rooms. Having exhausted that subject, Mrs Holland Burrage was silent for a moment before beginning again in an altered tone.

'And now, my dear,' she said, 'I must just put you on your guard against maintaining your intimacy with the McKendricks. If Lady Mary should offer you a home with her, you must be very delicate indeed about whom you introduce into her acquaintance, for she would be obliged, you know, to acknowledge them, which might be quite against her wishes. I have no doubt that the McKendricks will want you to perform the introduction, but you must make some excuse. They are good creatures, the very best creatures in the world, I dare say, but there's no denying they are *encroaching*.'

Eugenie had the misfortune to meet Marie's outraged

eye at that moment, and had difficulty in tearing her gaze away. She controlled the quivering of her lips with an effort, murmured a meek 'Yes, ma'am,' and thereafter fixed her eyes on the view of the horses' rumps and the regular rise and fall of the postillions seen through the forward window over her maid's shoulder.

The object of Mrs Holland Burrage's solicitude was at that moment regarding her nephew, the present Lord St Osyth, with some exasperation. There was no immediately apparent reason why the sight of him should cause anything but admiration to stir in an aunt's breast, for he was tall, well-formed, and exceedingly handsome, with glossy chestnut hair, hazel eyes, and beautifully sculpted features. To be sure, he was wearing top boots, the correctness of which for a morning visit in Town might be questionable, but the slightest trace of dust on their glossy surface suggested that he had ridden in from the country to pay the call, which would excuse him. The boots themselves were of the finest leather, and fitted his excellent calves to perfection. His buff-coloured broadcloth breeches, his coat of green Bath suiting, and his handsome Marseilles waistcoat proclaimed him a man of taste as well as of means; while his snowy linen, immaculately curled and pomaded locks, and perfectly manicured hands spoke of a certain natural fastidiousness.

Lady Mary, however, had nothing more tender to say to him than, 'Really, St Osyth, you are the most inconsiderate creature alive! It is a full three days since I sent for you, and now you arrive without warning at the most inconvenient time, when I am expecting visitors at every moment. I would be sure you did it deliberately to tease me, if I were not convinced you are interested in no one but yourself.'

Maximillian Freed, eighth Earl of St Osyth, raised an eyebrow at the words 'sent for you', and then resumed his normal expression of faintly amused hauteur, which went well with his posture as he lounged gracefully against the chimneypiece before the fire, one foot upon the fender, the better, it might be supposed, to display his well-developed thigh muscles. 'I beg your pardon, ma'am,' he said, not at all as if he wished to receive it. 'I have been out of Town this week past – at Freed, in fact – and finding your message awaiting me on my return, thought it best to delay my visit no longer. You see me,' he added with a graceful gesture of the hand towards his immaculate attire, 'in all my dirt.'

Lady Mary snorted. 'You have never ridden from Surrey in those clothes! It's of no use to try to bamboozle me, for I cut my teeth long ago. But how are things at Freed? It is always so beautiful at this time of year.' Her voice took on an eagerness as she spoke of her childhood home, and though there was no visible softening of her nephew's face, he spoke his next words more gently.

'You should go there, ma'am, and see for yourself. Go down for a visit, and stay as long as you like. There is no need to arrange it beforehand. I keep a small staff there, with instructions to be ready to receive me without notice at any time, and Mrs Bacon would see you were made comfortable. She enquired after you most warmly before I left this morning.'

'Dear Bacon! Do you know, St Osyth, she was house-keeper at Freed at the time of my wedding? She must be any age!'

'She is ageless, ma'am, like you,' he said with a bow.

Lady Mary's reminiscent eye hardened, and she searched her nephew's face for the sardonic gleam she was sure must be there. 'You like to amuse yourself at others' expense, but do not think you will draw me in. If that is your purpose in visiting me, you have wasted your time.'

St Osyth smiled. 'As I am here at your request, ma'am, I do not yet know my purpose in visiting you. Perhaps you will give yourself the trouble of enlightening me?'

'Certainly I will,' said Lady Mary vigorously. 'I wish to know when you mean to settle matters with Caroline

Stanley. Things have gone on long enough. It will not do to have people begin to talk.'

'And what matters, pray, am I to settle?' The hardness in St Osyth's voice would have warned any mortal less formidable than Lady Mary Berrington not to pursue the subject.

'Your marriage of course! Don't pretend to misunderstand me, St Osyth, for you are anything but stupid.' He bowed ironically at the compliment. 'It is high time you were married, and Lady Caroline is exactly right for you. A very good sort of young woman, and from the very best of families; and though Guisborough won't be able to provide her with a very handsome dowry, that cannot signify to you, placed as you are. Everyone has been expecting you to settle it this year past. I declare it is becoming quite embarrassing to meet Lady Guisborough's eye of late.'

St Osyth's face had steadily darkened through this speech, and though he maintained his overtly relaxed posture, there was now tension in every line of his athletic frame.

'I cannot think what has raised these expectations in you, ma'am. I have told you many times that I have no intention of marrying.'

'No *present* intention,' Lady Mary corrected him. 'You must marry sooner or later to provide yourself with an heir, and with things as they are, it cannot be too soon.'

'I already have an heir,' he replied evenly.

Lady Mary's mouth grew grim at this reference to her other nephew, her younger brother's son, the Honourable Sebastian Freed. 'Sebastian may be my nephew, but he is very far from being the sort of person I would wish to see in your position, Max. He is a mere fop, a – a macaroni. Besides, you cannot seriously expect me to believe that you would even consider allowing the title and estate to fall into the hands of a man who – who – '

'Who kicked your dog one Christmas in a fit of temper,'

St Osyth finished the sentence for her kindly. 'Well, no, I cannot say I should be very happy to think of his succeeding to my place.'

'Well, then – '

'But on the other hand,' he continued smoothly, 'I have no intention of marrying simply to please the family – or the Guisboroughs.'

'And what, pray, is your objection to Caroline Stanley?' Lady Mary enquired rigidly.

'I have nothing in common with her.'

'But you have known her from a child!'

St Osyth seemed to find that amusing. 'So have I many other young women. Am I to propose to them all?'

'Oh don't be tiresome! The Guisborough match is eligible in every way, the girl's parents want it, and everyone expects it. The whole of London waits only for you to make your offer.'

'The whole of London would have better minded its own business, and left me to mind mine,' he said with deceptive mildness. Two red spots appeared in Lady Mary's cheeks.

'Then what do you want, Max? You are two-and-thirty years old, and for the last fifteen of them every mother in the *ton* had been dangling her daughters in front of you, to no avail. London is full of unattached young women, many of them quite eligible, some of them pretty. What more do you want? Must you be so nice?'

'Yes,' he said, pushing himself upright and walking to the window. 'In this case, I believe I must. I am glad to serve you, ma'am, in any way possible, but in the question of choosing my wife I shall consider no one's wishes or tastes but my own; and if I cannot find the right woman, I shall not marry at all.'

'And leave Freed to Sebastian?'

'If necessary.'

'Pah! Romantical nonsense! In my day, a young man would have been ashamed to own to such selfishness! I blame my brother of course: he spoiled you wickedly from

61

the moment you were born. If he had had any notion at all of doing his duty, he would have betrothed you while you were still at school, and married you off before you had time to develop these fanciful notions. I suppose,' she concluded in a voice rich with scorn, 'you are hoping to fall in love?'

St Osyth did not rise to the bait. His attention had been drawn to the sight of a post chaise and four drawing up in the street outside. 'You said that you were expecting visitors, ma'am? I believe they have just arrived.' He turned from the window. 'I shall make my departure,' he said with a bow.

'Oh no, do not. Stay and meet her, Max, if you please. I am sure it will interest you. It is the great-niece of my childhood friend Alicie de Bohans. You remember I told you I had had a letter about her, the last time I saw you.'

'Oh yes, the young woman who escaped the guillotine,' St Osyth said. 'Now that, Aunt Mary, is very romantic indeed! She is penniless, I suppose, and seeking shelter with you until the monarchy is restored and she can return to her inheritance? But it is not like you, ma'am, to be swayed by stories of terrible misfortune and high adventure. I wish you may not be taken in.'

Lady Mary looked cross. 'I shall not be taken in, I assure you. I was extremely fond of Alicie – she was like a sister to me. If her great-niece is in distress, I must do what I can to help her; but nothing has been promised yet. If she is unsuitable, I shall give her some money and send her away, you may be sure.'

St Osyth said no more, and they waited in silence as the sounds of arrival were heard from below, followed by the measured tread of the butler ascending the stairs. A moment later he had opened the door wide, and announced with a sonority which revealed to his mistress, long versed in his mannerisms, that he approved of the visitor, 'The Countess de Talcy to see you, my lady.' He stood aside, and Eugenie stepped through the door, crossed the room to Lady Mary, and sank into a deep, respectful, and very graceful curtsey.

'Welcome, my dear,' said Lady Mary, and as the young woman rose and looked frankly into her face, she smiled warmly and said, 'So you are my dear Alicie's great-niece! Yes, you have a little the look of her: you have the de Bohans nose, at least. You would be sister Sophie's granddaughter, of course. I never met your grandmama, my dear, but Alicie often spoke of her, and told me in her letters about her marriage to de Talcy, and so on. And so your poor father is dead, I understand? Very sad for you, child, but a mercy he was not executed, at least. I am sure you feel it to be so.'

'Why yes, ma'am,' Eugenie said gravely. 'Papa always taught me that in every situation there is something to be glad about, if only one can find it out.'

St Osyth, standing by the window, had not yet seen the young woman full face, but so far he had not been impressed by her. Her figure was too small and thin to be imposing, though her carriage was graceful; and her attire was no more than neat and proper: there was nothing about her to attract admiration. But her reply to his aunt, perfectly serious in tone but, he was sure, concealing an undercurrent of ironic amusement, caught his attention. He stirred, and Lady Mary glanced at him, and then smiled at Eugenie.

'My dear, may I present to you my nephew, the Earl of St Osyth?' she said. Eugenie turned as he approached, but the light from the window being behind him, she was not able clearly to distinguish his features until he was close enough to take her hand, over which he bowed most correctly, and murmured an indifferent '*Enchanté*'.

Eugenie, who had turned quite white, executed a small, rigid curtsey. 'I 'ave not 'ad the pleasure of milord's acquaintance,' she said, losing her accent in her agitation, 'but I cannot say we 'ave not met before.'

St Osyth had released her hand and straightened up,

and he now surveyed her face with all the interest Mr Layton would display over half a yard of undyed calico. An eyebrow went up. 'I beg your pardon, ma'am?'

'On the London road, just outside Kingston,' Eugenie said evenly. 'You were so obliging as to look back after you had passed me in your curricle.'

For a moment he looked faintly puzzled, and then he appeared to recall the occasion. To Eugenie's fury, he betrayed no shame or regret, but merely turned a shrug into a slight bow and murmured, 'I regret I had forgotten the incident, ma'am.'

Lady Mary looked from one to the other. 'What is this? What do you say, Max?'

'Nothing of the least importance, Aunt,' St Osyth said with a faint smile.'And now, if you will forgive me, I will take my leave. I am sure you have a great deal to talk about. Your servant, ma'am . . .'

He bowed his way out, leaving Eugenie to swallow her confusion and fury, and to explain her outburst to Lady Mary as best she might.

Eugenie had been sufficiently confused before she entered the house; for when the post chaise drew up in front of the door, Mrs Holland Burrage had revealed that she had no intention of coming in with her.

'There can be no occasion for any more introduction, after all that has passed on the subject,' she said. 'Lady Mary will have a great many things to ask you, and it will be better for your first interview to be quite private. My acquaintance with her is slight, and she will not want to discuss family matters in front of me.'

All this was said in the kindest manner, and Eugenie felt ashamed of having misjudged her, and of feeling so relieved that the widow was not, after all, to pose as her sponsor. 'If you think it best, ma'am,' she assented.

'Aye, it won't do to look too eager,' Mrs Holland Burrage said decidedly, with a wag of her enormous turban. 'I shall take your luggage on to my house in Great Pulteney Street. It's only a few minutes from here, and when your interview is over, if Lady Mary don't care to have her horses put to, you may walk it easily with your maid. Lady Mary will send a footman along with you to show you the way. But of course she may ask you to stay, and then, you know, you may send a note round to me for your luggage.'

Everything Mrs Holland Burrage said spoke of good sense and propriety, and Eugenie, feeling her debt to the widow doubled by such delicacy, hardly knew how to thank her. She was admitted to Lady Mary's house by the butler, Treese – the first English butler she had encountered, and quite as formidable as she had always heard. He was expecting her. He asked her to follow him to the saloon where Lady Mary was waiting, and then sailed off majestically like a laden Spanish galleon. Eugenie only had time to bid Marie wait for her in the hall before following in his wake, up the handsome staircase to the first floor.

Lady Mary's reception of her had been everything that was kind, and had touched her deeply. The discovery that they were not alone, and that the intruding gentleman was none other than the traveller who had soaked her and then driven off without a word of apology, overset her completely. Her outburst was no sooner made than regretted, but the fact that it elicited no belated apology made it hard for her to contain her fury. It was fortunate that Lady Mary's curiosity about the incident was slight, for it would have been an unfortunate beginning to their relationship for Eugenie to reveal that she had conceived an implacable hatred and contempt for Lady Mary's nephew.

After his departure, however, Lady Mary reverted at once to more interesting topics. She required of Eugenie an account of her experiences and circumstances, and went on to relate the history of her own friendship with the de Bohans family. It was plain from the beginning that she had taken to Eugenie, for she spoke very freely to her, as if they had long enjoyed an intimate relationship.

'My papa, you see, was a great friend of the marquis, your great-grandpapa. They used to visit each other turn and turn about, and Papa took a great fancy to the de Bohans girls – there were three, you know, and all accounted great beauties, even in childhood. So he invited the marquis to send the eldest to be brought up at Freed. My dear Alicie! She was closer to me than my own sister, and I was heartbroken when she had to return home, but of course the marquis had arranged a match for her. He settled them all well – Alicie to de Narrandais, Sophie to de Talcy, and Elisabeth to the Duke of Gedenberg-Stolhessen – a good match, though he must have been thirty years her senior, and, as it turned out, unable to breed. Well, in the end, of the four of us, only Sophie produced an heir,' she mused. 'It was always a great sadness to Berrington and me that we had no children.'

'It is the will of God, madame,' Eugenie offered, as some comment seemed to be called for. Lady Mary regarded her thoughtfully.

'Is it, indeed? Well, that may be so, and it may be that it was God's will that you should arrive here just at this particular moment.'

'Madame?'

'You cannot know, of course,' Lady Mary continued, 'that my elderly cousin, who has lived with me since my dear husband's death, herself died last winter, leaving me without any companion. I have found myself very much confined, and since receiving the first news of your arrival in England, it has been in my mind, if I should find you to my liking, to offer you a home with me, as my companion and protégée. Now I have met you at last, and I do like you, very much. Should you like to come and live with me?'

'Oh, madame, indeed I would!' Eugenie cried. 'You are so very kind.'

'Nonsense, my dear. The truth is that I never had

a daughter, or even a niece, to launch into society, as I should have liked to do, and I fear my habits have become unnecessarily elderly. Having you here will be a great excuse for me to go into society again. The delights of the London Season! I have almost forgot them, though I used to be very gay in my young days. You had your come-out in Paris, I suppose?'

'Yes, ma'am. I was presented at Versailles,' Eugenie said. An unholy gleam entered Lady Mary's eye.

'At Versailles? Excellent! Oh, I shall very much enjoy bringing you to the attention of certain mamas of my acquaintance! I see the most underbred, ill-dressed young women nowadays pushed forward by their mothers. Manners, conduct, all lacking; no style, no refinement. You and I, my dear, will show them how it should be done!' She chuckled. 'Dear me, what a charming prospect! I feel quite exhilarated. How glad I am that you came to me, my dear child!'

Chapter Five

The news that Lady Mary Berrington had not only taken in a French emigrant as her protégée, but was preparing to come out of retirement in order to launch the young woman into society, was of the sort to arouse the deepest and most burning interest in those whose self-appointed duty it was to disseminate such news as rapidly as possible throughout fashionable London. Within hours of a footman's being sent round to Great Pulteney Street with a note for Mrs Holland Burrage, Lord St Osyth received a visit from his cousin and heir apparent, the Honourable Sebastian Freed, who was in a state of great excitement and indignation.

'Max – I say, Max, what's going on? What the deuce is Aunt Mary playing at? I shouldn't have believed a word of it, if I hadn't got it from Freddy Scawton – yes, and I must say, Max, it's too bad of you to tell him a thing like that and not me! Made it damned embarrassing for me. Deuce take it, he ain't family yet, you know!'

The Earl regarded his cousin with an air of mild enquiry, not unmingled with an element of sartorial criticism which would normally have roused the indignation of Mr Freed, who saw himself as the arbiter of fashion, and the most stylish dresser in Bond Street. St Osyth, however, as his satirical eye revealed, had serious misgivings about the suitability of a spangled shot-silk waistcoat for morning attire.

'My dear Sebastian, calm yourself, and tell me what you are talking about, for I haven't understood a word so far. What is it that the egregious Viscount Scawton has been so obliging as to lay at my door?'

'Why, this business of the Frenchwoman, of course,' Mr Freed said impatiently. 'Freddy says it's all over Town, so why haven't I heard anything about it? You may be going to marry his sister, but that doesn't mean – '

Lord St Osyth's eyes gleamed. 'Did Scawton tell you I was going to marry Caroline Stanley?'

'No – but everyone talks of it as a settled thing,' said Mr Freed carelessly.

'Then I should be obliged to you if you would advise the next person who talks of it as a settled thing in your hearing that I have not offered for Lady Caroline, that I have no intention of doing so, and that the engagement exists nowhere but in Lady Guisborough's mind.'

'Well, if that's true, I'm glad to hear it,' Mr Freed said cautiously, for though he was a lifelong companion in adversity of Viscount Scawton, he had no wish for Max to marry anyone, still less to see any part of the Freed fortune wasted in paying off the gambling debts of the bride's brother.

'Now, what is all this about the Frenchwoman?' St Osyth continued.

'*Don't* you know, then?' Freed asked in surprise. 'I thought you were at Brook Street this morning.'

'Good God, may I never move half a mile from my house without everyone's talking about it? I went to Berrington House at Lady Mary's request, and yes, I did meet the Comtesse there. What of it?'

'Freddy Scawton says Aunt Mary's taken this French-woman in to live with her, and means to adopt her as her daughter and leave her her fortune, that's what of it! I mean, Goddamnit, her whole fortune! Left to some

swarthy foreigner with no more claim upon her than –
than – '

'Than you have?' St Osyth suggested blandly. Mr Freed
had the grace to blush a little.

'Well, I'm her nephew. Who else would she leave it to?
You have as much as you can possibly want or need, Max;
and, yes, I don't deny that I've been relying on it. You
know how I'm situated. The Governor left me damnably
badly fixed when he quit his lease, and everyone's always
assumed that Aunt Mary would leave her fortune to me.'

'Everyone has had a great deal to say, one way and
another,' the Earl commented drily. Sebastian stirred rest-
lessly.

'Well?'

'Well what?'

'Is it true, damn it?'

The Earl raised an eyebrow. 'I haven't the least idea. If
it is, we will hear about it sooner or later from a more
informed source.'

Mr Freed muttered something which sounded disoblig-
ingly like 'damned cold fish' and picked up his cane,
preparatory to leaving. The Earl detained him.

'A word of advice, Sebastian. Two words. Firstly, that
Lady Mary is entitled to do anything she likes with her
fortune, and any adverse comment in public on your part
will only make you look foolish.' He watched his cousin
digesting the idea. 'Secondly – '

'Yes? You're always so full of good advice, Max,' Freed
said nastily.

'Such a pity you never take any of it,' St Osyth said
smoothly. 'My second piece of advice is that you stop
hoping for someone else to get you out of your financial
difficulties, and rely on your own abilities, which are not
negligible.'

'Much obliged to you,' Mr Freed said ironically, assum-
ing his hat. 'That's really valuable advice, from one who
has always lived by his wits.'

St Osyth was not provoked. 'I could have done so, had I needed to.'

'That's easy enough for you to say. You should try being me,' said Mr Freed bitterly. His cousin shuddered delicately.

'No thank you, Sebastian. You do it so well, I simply could not hope to emulate you.'

Mr Freed struggled for a moment, and then yielded an unwilling grin. That was the trouble with Max – he could always charm you out of the sullens, when he wanted to. 'Well, I'm off to Tatt's. That man of Freddy's has given me a sure-fire tip – can't lose. Do you dine at Brooks's tonight?'

'No, but I may look in later on.'

'I'll see you there, then – unless m'horse falls down,' cried Sebastian, and took his leave, swinging his cane cheerfully. He had the gambler's volatility of mood – and the eternal optimism, St Osyth reflected dourly, which he inherited from his father, whose ability to believe in one sure-fire tip after another had ensured he left his son nothing but debts.

When he entered the gaming room at Brooks's late that evening, St Osyth perceived straight away that, for once, the sure-fire tip had produced a result. The first person he saw was Sebastian, flushed of cheek and bright of eye, at the macao table, playing with much flourish and high spirits. Viscount Scawton was at his elbow, urging him on, and a number of others of their circle were making a great deal of noise and attracting to themselves the frowns of the serious-minded card players, engaged in the science of whist.

Before he could penetrate the room further, the Earl was arrested by the heavy hand of the Marquis of Guisborough, whose long face was more lugubrious even than usual.

'Ha! St Osyth, you here! Wanted to talk to you.' A loud whoop from the macao table distracted his attention, and he cast a mournful eye at his son and heir. 'That cub of mine, making a damned nuisance of himself, as usual. Blast his eyes, how he sings out! Castaway already, and it's barely past dinner time! He'll ruin me sooner or later, one way and another, that's for sure. Why can't he go to White's? Knows I prefer it here. I'd've black-balled him you know, only it was Grenville who put him up, and it don't do to look too particular.'

'Come, sir, isn't it better to have him here, where you can keep an eye on him?' St Osyth said with amusement.

Guisborough grunted. 'Maybe so. But I come here for peace and quiet, not to watch that boy squandering my fortune, damn it.'

'Buy him a pair of colours, then,' St Osyth said. 'He's been asking for long enough. A spell abroad would do him good.'

'Can't,' Guisborough said gloomily. 'Lady G. won't hear of it while he's single. Until he's wed and got himself an heir, everything hangs on him – only son, damn it, and I've no brothers. For m'self, I'd like nothing better than to pack him off to the Low Countries, but we can't take the risk of him getting killed in action.'

The conversation seemed treacherously to have turned itself round to the one topic above all others St Osyth was anxious to avoid with Guisborough, and he sought for a neutral comment to keep it at bay.

'The rooms are crowded tonight. I don't recognise half of the company.'

'Pah! Place is going to the dogs, if you ask me,' said Guisborough at once. 'Strangest people seem to get in. Who's that fellow, for instance, next to Freddy? Queer-looking cove – seems to know you, St Osyth,' he added as the gentleman in question caught St Osyth's eye and bowed. The Earl hesitated before offering the slightest inclination of the head which might charitably be construed as a return of the compliment, revealing that if he acknowledged, he certainly did not welcome, the acquaintance.

'His name is Lambert Beecham,' St Osyth said tersely.

'I just know him – a nodding acquaintance. But what was it you wanted to speak to me about, sir?' he added, revealing that the new topic was even more unwelcome than the other.

'Eh? Oh, yes – wanted you to satisfy my curiosity. Well, Lady G.'s, to be precise. Word is that some long-lost relative of yours has turned up from overseas and is putting up with your aunt, Lady Mary Berrington. Thing is,' he continued hastily, as a more than usually frigid look overcame the Earl's face at this apparently impertinent curiosity, 'We're givin' a dinner next week, and Lady Mary's guest of honour, and Lady G. wanted to know if she ought to send along a card for this other young lady. Wouldn't like to be behindhand with any compliment, you know.'

'You are most obliging, sir,' St Osyth countered with his most sarcastic smile. 'I'm sure if Lady Guisborough were to refer the enquiry to Lady Mary, her curiosity would be satisfied. And now, if you will forgive me – your servant, sir.'

It was not the last time that evening that St Osyth was obliged to fend off the curiosity of his fellow members, and his politeness grew more frigid as the evening wore on. The coldest of his manners were reserved, however, for the approach of that Lambert Beecham whom Guisborough had described as a 'queer-looking cove'. Beecham was a man of moderate height and slender build, dark and sallow-skinned. His face was pitted by the scars of a childhood skin disease, which evidently made it difficult for him to shave, for his heavy beard showed blue around his jowls, and here and there a crop of short black bristles sprouted from a seam where the razor could not reach. His lips were full, and looked rather indecently red and naked in all that hirsute darkness. His black eyebrows were densely bushy over small, very dark eyes, whose orbits were curiously bistred, probably as the result of some past illness. He was correctly dressed in evening clothes, but his powdered hair was such a startling contrast to his extreme swarthiness that it seemed a bizarre jest, as though he had decided to draw attention to what could not be concealed. He approached St Osyth without smiling, not ingratiatingly, but with a curious sly confidence, like a cur-dog approaching the butcher's stall.

St Osyth addressed him impatiently. 'Well, Beecham, what have you to say to me?'

'I understand I have to offer you congratulations, my lord, on the acquisition of a new relative?' Beecham said.

St Osyth's lip curled. 'You can offer nothing which I would accept.'

The black eyes watched him consideringly. 'Oh come, now, that isn't very friendly to a fellow member. And not entirely true, either; isn't there a little matter of a gold snuff box? Don't tell me, sir, that you wouldn't accept *that* if I were to offer it?'

'You acquired that snuff box by foul means, Beecham. My cousin was drunk – '

'Drunk or not, my lord, I won it in a fair wager. I have witnesses to that.'

'I'm sure you have,' St Osyth said angrily. 'You knew, however, that the snuff box belonged to me, and that Freed had no right to wager it, and yet you still took it.'

'Such a pretty thing,' Beecham said, almost with a smile. 'A family heirloom, so I understand – and the miniature painted on the lid – your grandmother? Yes, I thought so. You must be very anxious to get it back, Earl – particularly as your cousin must have abstracted it from your house by, shall we say, unconventional means?'

'I have already offered to redeem it,' St Osyth said shortly, and Beecham cut in smoothly.

'Oh yes, but for the amount of the original wager only. Not very handsome of you, when it must be worth ten times that at least, not even taking into account the sentimental value. Besides, I took a fancy to it at the time. I'm quite willing to let you have it back, but I feel I ought to be compensated for its loss. I don't wish to be greedy, however. Shall we say three thousand pounds? That seems fair to me.'

St Osyth's face darkened. 'That's blackmail, plain and simple. By God, I ought to horsewhip you!'

Now Beecham's face changed too, an ugly anger and resentment boiling up from some deep reservoir within him. 'And I ought to call you out, for daring to speak thus to a gentleman – '

'You are not a gentleman, however, and I would not dignify you by accepting a challenge, even if you were rash enough to issue it,' St Osyth said contemptuously. 'I suppose your gambling debts are grown so heavy you thought you could recoup the situation by trying to blackmail me. But I tell you, Beecham, you have chosen the wrong victim!'

'And I warn you, St Osyth, that you badly underestimate me. I know a great deal more about the affairs of your family than you think, and you would do well to consider before you make an enemy of me.' With these words Beecham turned on his heel and walked away, back towards the macao table, where St Osyth saw, with anger and misgivings, that he at once attached himself to Sebastian Freed in the most friendly and encouraging manner.

That young fool! the Earl apostrophised him silently. The affair of the snuffbox was the latest in a series of incidents in which Sebastian had revealed how little judgement and how few scruples he had. He was an expensive young man, and having been spoiled throughout his youth by an adoring mother, he had come to regard his present impecuniosity as an unnatural state which it was everyone else's duty to relieve. He borrowed money wherever he could, with no hope and only the haziest intentions of repaying his debts; he gambled with no regard for the family's reputation; he pledged money he did not have, and expected St Osyth, as head of the family, to honour his pledges; and recently, and most disastrously, he had abstracted from Freed a number of small but valuable items which, as heirlooms, he considered to be practically his own property.

'They'll come to me eventually,' he reasoned. 'I am the heir, and they'll do me more good now than they will at some date in the future.'

St Osyth had discreetly managed to retrieve most of them, except for the gold snuffbox Sebastian had put up as collateral in some drunken wager and lost to the sinister Beecham, a man who lived on the fringes of good society, making a precarious living from his skill with dice and cards. That he also practised a refined form of blackmail St Osyth now had evidence; and he would not have been surprised to learn that Beecham was involved in other more definitely criminal activities.

The Earl was angry to see Sebastian apparently on friendly terms with him, but knew that to remonstrate would only be likely to make Sebastian more determined to maintain the intimacy. Later in the evening, when the opportunity came to speak to Sebastian, the Earl asked him what he and Beecham had been talking about. To his surprise, it was not the snuffbox.

'Oh, he was asking me about Aunt Mary Berrington's new companion,' said Sebastian easily. 'Seems he knows a lot of French people, wondered if she was a friend or relation of any of them. Spouted a lot of French names at me. Went on and on – rather a bore.'

'What names? Do you remember any of them?' St Osyth asked.

Sebastian looked amazed. 'My dear St Osyth, I couldn't have pronounced half of 'em, let alone remember 'em. Foreign jawbreakers! Suppose this woman of Aunt Mary's is the same. *I* couldn't tell him her name.'

'He asked her name?'

'Didn't I just say so? Ah, here's Freddy looking for me,' said Sebastian, and ambled away leaving his cousin to ponder the significance of Beecham's curiosity, and to conclude that he was looking for some new way to cause trouble. It seemed unlikely that the Frenchwoman would have any dark secrets to hide, but all the same, St Osyth thought it would be wise to be on his guard in every direction, and he made a mental note to enter into conversation with her at the first opportunity, and find out what he could.

As the first step in introducing Eugenie to society, Lady Mary decided to give an evening party for a few select friends. Eugenie had been in London a week before this event took place, and already gossip was rife and the most extraordinary stories were circulating about her, some of which she learnt from the lips of Mrs Holland Burrage when she paid the widow a morning visit at Great Pulteney Street.

'Well, my dear, you have fallen on your feet, and no mistake! Of course, I detest gossip, and never pay the least attention to it, but I must say if only half what I hear about you is true, then you have got your head in the creampot all right. How do you like Lady Mary?'

'Oh, she is everything that is good,' Eugenie said. 'She treats me with such kindness, as though she were my aunt.'

'Ah yes, so they are saying,' Mrs Holland Burrage nodded significantly. 'And who knows? After all, Berrington was a warm man, and she has no chick or child to spend her fortune on. Of course, there are the two nephews; but the one, so they say, is an unsatisfactory sort of young man, and the other – ' She gave Eugenie a thoughtful look. 'Have you met the Earl, her nephew?'

'Yes, ma'am – he was there when I first arrived,' said Eugenie neutrally.

'A handsome man, wouldn't you say? Not that it would signify if he were as ugly as a gargoyle, for he's one of the richest men in England, and unwed, though he was supposed to have been all but engaged to Guisborough's antidote of a daughter this year and more. But by what I hear, he has broke off that connection just this last week – since you arrived at Berrington House, by coincidence. Now what do you say to that, miss?'

Eugenie looked distressed. 'It is coincidence, ma'am. How could it be anything more?'

'Oh, as to how, I don't pretend to know all the gossips claim to, with their nods and half-sentences and *I-would-if-I-coulds*. But Lady Mary's fortune is not to be sneezed at, and she may leave it where she will. And no man is so rich, that he would willingly forgo a tidy little sum he has always counted on as his own.'

Eugenie understood enough of what the widow was suggesting to wish she spoke English less well. 'I 'ave met 'im only once, madame,' she said in distress. 'We nodded to each other. He seems to me a very cold man. I did not like 'im, I confess.'

'Now child, don't upset yourself,' said Mrs Holland Burrage, patting Eugenie's knee. 'I'm only telling you what people are saying. I don't suppose there's a grain of truth in it. But if there should be, I only wish to put you on your guard, so that you can make the best of the opportunity. After all, you're an earl's daughter yourself, even though it's only a foreign earl, and there are more unequal matches made every day of the week. There's no smoke without fire, so they say, and if he's been asking questions about you, it stands to reason – '

'Asking questions?'

'Yes, of our old friend McKendrick amongst others, which was how I got to hear of it. You can be sure McKendrick will have painted you in the best light, so there's nothing to worry about there. But, now, do behave pleasantly towards him when you next meet him, for you know first impressions count, as I've told you before, and if you was to put him off with any little awkwardness, there's no knowing but he'd change his mind.'

Though upset at the time, Eugenie was soon able to dismiss what Mrs Holland Burrage had said as the idlest of idle gossip. That the Earl had no particular interest in her was proved by the fact that after their first, brief meeting, he did not again call in Brook Street, though there was a constant stream of morning visitors who came to pay their compliments to the dowager and to stare at Eugenie. The 'unsatisfactory' nephew was one, and though on his first visit he looked at Eugenie with an ill-concealed, if inexplicable hostility, he did not fail to call again twice more in the next three days, during which visits his initial dislike of her seemed to be undergoing a transmutation into admiration.

Any further acquaintance with the Earl had to wait until the evening party; and Eugenie, with a growing affection for Lady Mary and strong feelings of gratitude towards her, was willing to give her senior nephew a second chance to redeem himself. If he apologised in due form for his previous behaviour, she was prepared to forgive him most handsomely, and even to like him from then on. By dwelling inwardly on the prospect while sewing her new gown for the evening party, she had created in her mind a very pleasing scene of his contrition, her generosity, and their future cousinly affection for each other. As she stood beside Lady Mary on the evening of the party, becomingly gowned in apricot silk with her hair dressed simply but effectively with gold ribbons, she awaited the Earl's arrival with pleasant anticipation, as one might await the entry on stage of the hero in a favourite play.

The time for receiving passed, however, without his appearance, and as Lady Mary moved away from the door of the saloon to mingle with her guests, she complained *sotto voce* to her protégée: 'Max is the most inconsiderate creature alive! He lives for nothing but pleasure, and thinks of no one but himself. I particularly wanted him to be here early tonight, and now I suppose he will not arrive until eleven and stay only ten minutes. No doubt he is engaged in one of his dreadful schemes! He will come in and bow and say nothing more than "I'm sorry, I was delayed by business", as if we didn't all know what his business was! He is just like his father – all thoughtlessness and extravagance. The money he throws away on those creatures! But here is Lady Grantham – I had better say no more, for fear of shocking her.'

Eugenie could only consent, and was left with a mind reeling from the new ideas she had received about the Earl. Thoughtless – extravagant – given to 'dreadful schemes'? And who were the 'creatures' on whom he squandered his money, whose existence would shock Lady Grantham? She was afraid she could guess only too well, and it boded ill for her plan of reconciliation. In France, a gentleman would be ashamed to allow his female relatives to understand anything of his private *arrangements*. The Earl of St Osyth must have behaved with a grave lack of delicacy for his aunt to be so distressingly well aware of them; and that, alas, would accord with the unfavourable opinion Eugenie had early formed of him.

The Earl was announced at last, not quite at eleven o'clock, but certainly well after any hour which could have been accounted for by any normal delay. By that time, Eugenie would not have been surprised if he had presented himself in riding dress, but he was properly clad in evening attire, immaculate from the powdered wig to the gold shoe buckles, and looking, had she been in a fit state to notice it, very handsome. She saw him approach Lady Mary and make his bow and, presumably, his excuses. Then he looked around him slowly, his eye travelling lordly-wise around the crowded room like a sultan surveying an unpromising batch of newly captured Circassian slaves. Eugenie found herself beginning to seeth inwardly, and when his cool eye finally rested on her, she turned away so that she might not meet it.

Nevertheless, he had seen her, and the etiquette of the

evening demanded he present himself to her, and he began to make his way across the room towards her, his progress delayed only by the courtesies he was obliged to exchange with the various elderly ladies of his aunt's acquaintance. He reached Eugenie and made his bow, and looked her over as she rose from her curtsey with a frankness which in other circumstances she would have admired, but which now appeared to her as bordering on impertinence.

'Well, ma'am, I trust I find you well? You certainly present a very changed appearance from our first meeting. The change becomes you very well, I might say.'

'Indeed, sir? You had so much difficulty, when last we met, in remembering the occasion of our first meeting, that I should not have thought you would be able to make any comparison,' Eugenie said with a rigidly pleasant smile.

St Osyth raised an eyebrow. 'You aren't still brooding on *that* are you, you foolish child?'

'Foolish child I may be, but I have an excellent memory, my lord,' Eugenie countered, 'and I do not remember that ever you apologised for drenching me and my maid in such a callous way.'

'Apologise?' he said with an evident astonishment which only served to make Eugenie more angry. 'What should I apologise for? You don't think I did it on purpose, do you?'

'That I cannot tell. But the puddle was very large and plain to be seen, and anyone driving with normal care and attention would have seen it and avoided it.'

He shrugged. 'I was in a great hurry that day. I was driving fast, as you no doubt noticed, and had no time to be looking out for puddles.'

'Or for ladies walking by the roadside,' said Eugenie, seething, 'though you were so very obliging as to look back for a moment, when I cried out. Yes, you looked back, but you did not stop.'

'My good child, I saw no ladies!' St Osyth said, infuriatingly reasonable. 'I saw only what I took to be two women of the lower orders trudging along; and dressed as you were, what else was I to think?'

'Oh, I am sure that if you had thought I was a gentle-woman, you would have stopped.'

'Then what have I done amiss? You really cannot mean to be taking offence because I did not see through your disguise and immediately recognise you as a lady of quality!'

'No, my lord, I do not. But if you thought I was a pauper, the more shame on you not to have stopped, for to soak the dress of such a person, who would have no other to change into, and probably no means of drying it, was to inflict greater hardship than ever you could inflict on a lady.'

She saw that she had struck home with that, for two red spots of shame or anger flared in his cheeks. But he only looked more aloof than ever, and said in an amused voice, 'Why, ma'am, these are dangerously egalitarian opinions to be espousing in an English drawing room! I should have thought it was just such revolutionary ideas which caused your flight from France.'

'It is nothing of the sort,' Eugenie snapped. 'My father fought the revolution until he died, but he taught me always to have consideration for those less fortunate than myself. That is simply good manners.'

Now she had offended him. 'I must thank you, ma'am, for teaching me my manners when I had so evidently forgot them,' he said with a frigid bow. 'But I see how it is: you are angry with me not for my original offence, but for not apologising when I met you here at my aunt's. But I must tell you that I do not apologise where I do not believe myself at fault; therefore you must excuse me.'

'Ah, if you were not wrong before, you are wrong now!' Eugenie cried in a low, intense voice. For a moment he met her eyes, startled out of his languid pose into meeting her gaze person to person, frankly, with no disguise. The moment extended itself perilously, and she saw a change come over him. She did not know what it was, but suddenly he was looking at her differently, as though he knew her from some previous encounter, and something stirred in her, and she felt her cheeks growing warm and her heart beating faster.

Then it was over. The veil dropped before his eyes again, and with a slight, cool bow he walked away, leaving her angry, resentful, but most of all confused.

Chapter Six

Lady Mary very soon had the pleasure of knowing her scheme successful. Eugenie's pretty manners and respectful bearing towards her elders made her immediately acceptable to the high-sticklers amongst society hostesses who deplored modern informality. Those who wished for consequence were attracted by her title and the fact that it was Lady Mary Berrington who was sponsoring her, while the gayer set appreciated her pleasant smile, twinkling eye, and general air of chic. Each day following the evening party brought a new batch of invitations, while a constant stream of visitors to Berrington House brought a new spriteliness to the butler's ancient legs. In short, as Lady Mary observed with satisfaction to her maid, it was clear that Eugenie had 'taken'.

The Honourable Sebastian seemed bent on furthering his acquaintance with her, and at an early date engaged to take her for a drive in the Park. To anyone unacquainted with his way of life it would have seemed a small enough undertaking, but in fact it entailed exertions which amounted almost to heroism, for not only had he to rise two hours earlier than was his usual habit on the day itself, but he was obliged to spend the better part of two evenings beforehand attempting to persuade various friends to lend him a curricle or phaeton and the horses to draw it. Sebastian was known amongst his acquaintance as a Smart, a Tulip of fashion, and up to every rig as far as Town bronze was concerned; but not even those who loved him best could claim that he handled the reins with any great skill, and his closest friends suffered from a deep reluctance to entrust their paintwork or their cattle to him.

In the end, to Sebastian's astonishment as much as anyone's, it was St Osyth who came to his rescue, with the offer of his curricle and a pair of chestnuts which many a Whip would have given his eyeteeth to own. Sebastian was reduced almost to speechlessness.

'I s-say, Max – are you sure? It's damned good of you! I – I don't know what to say.'

St Osyth gave him a glance of lazy amusement. 'The offer is not unconditional. Firstly, you must come out with me this afternoon, so that I can see you perform, and if you once job my horses' mouths, I'll withdraw the loan at once. And secondly, you must take my groom, Buckland, with you when you drive in case anything should happen, and take his advice on all things.'

'Of course, of course, old fellow,' Sebastian said placatingly. 'Anything you say. And you needn't worry – I'll treat 'em like eggshells! But I can't understand – I mean, I didn't think I was exactly in your good books recently – '

'Just call it cousinly affection,' St Osyth cut in smoothly. 'I shall probably take a ride myself on the Great Day, to see how you get on.'

Sebastian could only conclude that Max was playing some deep game of his own, as was usually the case, and as the conclusion released him from the need to feel any overpowering gratitude, he was happy to let it stand. On the morning of the proposed drive, the good Buckland brought the rig round to Sebastian's lodgings in Ryder Street, and Sebastian, with infinite care, uncomfortably aware of the groom's critical eye on him, then drove to Brook Street.

Eugenie was waiting for him, becomingly attired in a smart emerald-green pelisse and hat and a very dashing new pair of half-boots. Lady Mary inspected her appearance minutely when she came into the morning room, and pronounced herself satisfied.

'The boots are very well. You have a pretty ankle, my dear, and nothing sets off a pretty ankle so well as a half-boot.'

'Indeed, I am very grateful to you, ma'am,' Eugenie began, but Lady Mary waved away her thanks.

'I always think it the greatest folly to economise on boots. Besides, your making your own clothes is a great economy to me, for London mantuamakers must be the most expensive in the world, I am sure, and often unsatisfactory. In my girlhood, when I lived in the country, we always had our gowns made up at home; but my present maid has not the least skill with the needle, I'm afraid.'

'Marie and I would be very glad to make anything for you, ma'am, if you should like it,' Eugenie said, upon which Lady Mary's smile positively beamed.

'You know, my dear, your appearance lacks but one thing. If you will permit, I shall send Hoskins upstairs to fetch down my sable tippet and muff. A fur makes all the difference when the morning air is chilly, and sable is quite the thing this season. They will look very well against that green velvet.'

So Eugenie went downstairs and was handed into the curricle looking not only very smart, but elegantly prosperous too, with the black fur tippet brushing her cheeks, and her hands buried deep in the enormous muff. Buckland, holding the chestnuts' heads, gave her a covert look of approval. He had taken care to exercise them well that morning before driving to Ryder Street, so that they should be quiet enough for Mr Sebastian to handle. He was fiercely proud of his master's rigs and horses, and hated to think of their being let down by inferior human beings, but Miss's appearance reassured him, and when she smiled a courteous greeting to him and cast an eager and appreciative eye over the glossy pair, he felt an unusual warmth stirring in his breast. To his mind, true gentility was revealed by a person's courtesy to dependants and an appreciation of fine horseflesh. Miss having displayed both in that instant, he was willing to forgive his master for having allowed Mr Sebastian to borrow the curricle and pair in the first place.

Eugenie, who had put Sebastian down as a mere fribble, was agreeably surprised by the evident quality of his horses and respectability of his groom, and expressed herself politely on the subject. Aware of Buckland being within earshot, Sebastian had reluctantly to tell her the truth.

'The fact is the rig ain't mine. Belongs to m'cousin – you know, St Osyth. I don't keep any horses myself – don't have my own establishment, so it never seemed worth it,' he added in hurried explanation.

Eugenie was intrigued. 'Did the Earl lend this to you especially to take me out this morning? That was very kind of him.'

'Well, it was,' Sebastian said, his voice revealing his surprise in a way which endeared him to Eugenie more than sophistication could. 'He don't usually let anyone drive his cattle – dashed particular about 'em – and to say truth, I'm not his favourite relative at the moment. Max is as good a fellow as ever lived, but he's a high-stickler, as bad as Aunt Mary in his own way, and the fact of the matter is he's never approved of me.' This hardly accorded with the view Eugenie had received of the earl as an expensive libertine, and she expressed a delicate enquiry as to the reason for his disapproving of his cousin. Sebastian shrugged. 'Oh, it's often the way, you know,' he said with a worldly-wise air. 'Those that used to be rips when they were young are the worst of all when they reform. Go to the other extreme, you know, and try to stop everyone else enjoying 'emselves!'

A slight sound from behind reminded Sebastian that Buckland was listening to every word, and he changed the subject hastily by pointing out the various notable buildings they were passing. 'And here we are at the

Park gates, you see. This is the fashionable place to ride and drive. I expect you had somewhere like this in Paris?'

'Oh yes, in the Bois de Boulogne,' Eugenie said, a little wistfully. 'It seems so long since I was last there. Papa and I used to ride there together. When I was fifteen he bought me the prettiest bay mare, my darling Noisette. How I cried when I had to part with her!'

'Oh, you ride, then?' Sebastian asked with interest.

'There is nothing I like better,' she said with a smile, 'though it seems to me,' looking round her at the sedate progress everyone was forced to make on the crowded carriageway, 'that there is not much riding to be done in such a fashionable place.'

'Lord, no! When we want a good gallop, we go to Richmond Park. One comes here only to be seen and nod to one's friends,' said Sebastian frankly. 'You'd no more come to the Park for a ride than you'd go to the theatre to see a play.'

'I think you are very satirical,' Eugenie said severely. 'But how pleasant the sunshine is! I am almost too hot in these furs.'

Sebastian glanced at them shrewdly. 'Aunt Mary must have taken to you prodigiously to lend you her sables. Sir Arthur gave her the tippet and muff one birthday, and that maid of hers, Hoskins, took 'em to bed with her every night for the first six months, so Max says, to make sure they were safe.'

'Lady Mary is very kind,' Eugenie agreed warmly, not unaware of a more particular curiosity on Sebastian's part which politeness prevented him from expressing. 'And here is your cousin, if I mistake not,' she added, seeing the earl riding towards them on a good-looking bay. 'How very opportune that we should meet him here.'

'Nothing of the sort,' said Sebastian shortly. 'Said he'd be here, to keep an eye on me. Deuced sharp eye, too! See him lookin' me over, as if he thought I was ruining his chestnuts' mouths? He might as well tell everyone he

89

passes I'm a bad driver as look at me like that! Still,' he remembered belatedly, 'kind of him to lend me the rig. Hullo, Max! Fancy meetin' you here!'

'Sebastian – your servant, ma'am,' St Osyth greeted them shortly as he reined in beside them. His eyes met his groom's briefly and apparently received some reassurance from them, for his smile at once grew more cordial. 'A pleasant day for a drive, is it not?'

'Indeed, my lord,' said Eugenie, 'and your horses go very sweetly. You must keep them very well exercised.'

He gave her a sharp look, and then laughed. 'So Sebastian has told you all, has he? I admire you for your honesty, cousin. It will do you no harm with the countess, I assure you. She admires honesty above all things – am I not right, mademoiselle?'

'It is one of the things I admire,' she replied reservedly.

'I'm glad you have come along, Max,' Sebastian said eagerly, 'for now you've seen how I manage your pair, I'm hoping you might lend me one of your riding horses. Lady Eugenie has expressed a desire to go riding in Richmond Park, and I should like to arrange it for her.'

St Osyth's eyes flickered over Eugenie with new interest. 'You like to ride, ma'am?'

'Very much,' she said. 'I was brought up with horses. Though Papa lived so much in Paris, he was fond of riding, and taught me when I was quite a little girl.'

'Then we must see to it that you are provided with a mount,' St Osyth said. Not only the words, but the tone was kind, and Eugenie looked at him, a little puzzled, for she had expected him to be still offended with her. His expression, as always, was guarded and difficult to penetrate, but when she met his eyes they seemed to her watchful and speculative. She had no idea what he was thinking, but she had no doubt that in offering to lend her a horse he had some end in view which had nothing to do with her pleasure. To her annoyance she felt herself blushing, and was searching for a polite way of refusing him, when a diversion presented itself in the arrival of a large barouche containing a number of fashionably dressed ladies, which drew up beside them, entirely blocking the carriageway.

'Ah, St Osyth! There you are!' came the penetrating voice of the largest and most senior of the ladies in the barouche. Lady Guisborough was an ample and heavily dressed woman of advanced but vigorous years, who had never allowed her husband's unfortunate financial circumstances affect her assumption that the world had been created for her personal benefit. She had an expensive and profligate son and four plain daughters, but she never forgot that the Stanleys were second in consequence only to her own family, who traced their lineage back to the Plantagenets.

Beside her in the carriage was her eldest daughter, Lady Caroline, who at twenty had been out for four years without ever having attracted the attentions of any man Lady Guisborough would consider accepting for her. Caroline had been unfortunate in inheriting her father's rather long and lugubrious face and her mother's shallow and colourless eyes, while her upbringing had seen to it that in company she never had anything to say for herself which might overcome her lack of physical charms. Lady Guisborough never considered these matters. Marriages were arranged by parents between offspring who were suited to each other by blood and connections, nothing else. It was to be deplored that St Osyth had lost both his parents and come so early into his title and estate that he had acquired an unfortunate independence of thought and manner; but Lady Guisborough did not allow herself to be discouraged. The previous Earl had spoken approvingly of the match when Maximillian was at Eton and Caroline still in the cradle, and as far as she was concerned, that was as good as a betrothal.

Opposite her on the forward seats were her second and third daughters, Lady Maud and Lady Beatrix. Both were a little prettier than their elder sister, though not by much. Lady Maud was eighteen and plump; and Lady Beatrix, just out, was sixteen and had spots. Maria, the youngest, was fifteen and still in the schoolroom, and as she was the plainest of the four, she was naturally supposed to be the clever one of the family. Lady Guisborough had stated so often and so firmly that Maria was clever, that even Maria herself now believed it.

'Well, St Osyth, I'm glad to see you out and takin' some healthy exercise,' Lady Guisborough boomed as the Earl performed the difficult feat of bowing from horseback with remarkable grace. 'I don't hold with young men frowstin' in bed until all hours. Mr dear Papa rose from his bed at five o'clock in summer and six o'clock in winter every day of his life. I'm always tellin' Scawton the same – and that young cousin of yours should take heed of my advice. Early to bed and early to rise – that was always the way in my family!' She turned her basilisk stare on Sebastian, who, reflecting that Lady Guisborough's notoriously mutton-headed father had died both prematurely and bankrupt, was unable to prevent himself from emitting a weak giggle. The disapproval of the stare intensified. 'What, is the boy feeble-minded, St Osyth?'

'I fear it may be so, ma'am,' the Earl said with a sigh. 'There is a streak of it in the best families.'

'True,' said Lady Guisborough, nodding her enormous hat solemnly. 'Had two cousins and an uncle a little weak in the attic. Nothin' in that to be ashamed of. In fact, I don't entirely trust a man who's too clever. Somethin' not quite gentlemanly about it. I'd sooner a man had good connections than good brains. Never encouraged any of *my* children to read a book.' The thought seemed to strike her, and she waved a hand over the carriage. 'Here are my girls, you see, St Osyth! Caroline, say good mornin' to the Earl.' Caroline complied faintly, and the Ladies Maud and Beatrix clutched each other and giggled. 'You see,' said Lady Guisborough triumphantly, 'nothin' brainy about my

92

girls. Blood, that's what they've got! Lord! you don't ask a horse questions before you breed it, do you?'

Sebastian by now was biting the insides of his cheeks, but St Osyth's countenance was perfectly controlled, grave and courteous. 'Indeed you don't, ma'am,' he assented. The marchioness seemed satisfied. 'Well, you may present the young woman to me,' she said with a nod. 'I suppose this is the de Bohans girl I've been hearin' about? My grandpapa knew the old marquis, when he was in England, of course; we Clevelands never go abroad. Does she speak English? I don't hold with foreign languages. No call for anyone to speak anythin' but English, that I've ever understood!'

St Osyth gave Eugenie a quick and warning glance as he presented her. 'The Comtesse de Talcy, ma'am.'

'Glad to make your acquaintance,' Lady Guisborough said graciously as Eugenie bowed. 'Countess, eh? Your father was an earl, I take it?'

'Yes, madame,' said Eugenie.

'We don't do things that way in England,' Lady Guisborough told her. 'Still, there's no harm in it, I suppose. Left all your fortune behind in France, so they say. Your father went to the guillotine, I collect?' Her two younger daughters gave a strangled gasp at the words, and clutched each other again in gratified horror.

Eugenie, controlling herself admirably, replied, 'No, ma'am, he died of natural causes.'

'No shame on him if he had,' Lady Guisborough pronounced. 'However, it's just as well perhaps. Well, here are my daughters, you see, Caroline, Maud, Beatrix. You may tell Lady Mary I'll come and call on her soon, and bring 'em with me. You will like to become better acquainted with them. They are just your sort of girls.' Eugenie could make no reply to this but another bow, but Lady Guisborough didn't seem to notice. 'Seems a pretty-behaved sort of young woman,' she observed to St Osyth, just as if Eugenie were not two yards away from her. 'Pity she's no fortune. Bound to affect her prospects, her bein' a foreigner; though Lady Mary's patronage will help a little. She might still make a respectable sort of marriage. Well, St Osyth, I shall move along now. You must come and dine with us next week. Tuesday would be best. I'll tell Guisborough to arrange it with you. Good morning to you. Selley, drive on!'

The space and silence caused by the removal of the marchioness's barouche was so large that it amounted almost to a vacuum, and for a moment the three left behind felt too dazed and breathless to speak. Then Sebastian began to giggle again. 'Lord, Max! She has you sewn up all right and tight. You'll find yourself leg-shackled to that fright of a daughter of hers yet!'

'Hold your tongue,' said St Osyth shortly. Sebastian ignored the advice.

'I never thought to see you so meek and compliant! "Yes ma'am, no ma'am"! And tellin' you when you was to go and dine with her. Next Tuesday's the day, all right! After dinner, Guisborough will take you into his smoking room, give you a cigar, and name the day. I wish you very happy, Max. After all, it's blood, not brains or beauty, that counts!'

'When you have quite finished amusing yourself at my expense,' St Osyth said acerbicly, 'you might like to consider that while a measure of politeness and forbearance is due to elderly ladies of rank, I am under no such restraint with Guisborough. I can assure you I shan't be dining there next Tuesday, or any other day next week.'

Sebastian chuckled. 'I shouldn't like to bet on that.'

'Mr Freed,' Eugenie interposed, 'it is most unfair of you to tease your cousin simply because he is polite to her ladyship. He showed the greatest forbearance. You should rather admire him than laugh at him.'

'Oh, very well,' Sebastian said with a grin, 'only I shall admire him even more if he goes on being forbearing when Lady G. is his mama-in-law!'

'He is incorrigible, ma'am. It is not worth your while to

94

waste any more breath on him,' St Osyth said to Eugenie. He looked at her a little quizzically. 'It was very kind of you to give me your support, however.'

Eugenie did not want him to think she had forgiven him, just because she recognised that he had behaved as he ought towards Lady Guisborough. 'I am sure you have always known what is due to ladies of *rank*, my lord,' she said sweetly, and saw the gentler light disappear from his eyes as he gave her an ironical bow in reply.

'I must not detain you any further,' he said abruptly, gathering his reins. At that moment, another horseman passing by turned his head to look keenly at Eugenie, and raised his hat to the two gentlemen, a courtesy which they both returned, Sebastian self-consciously, and St Osyth coldly. Eugenie, however, had turned a little pale.

'That man,' she said breathlessly, 'who is he? Why did he stare at me so?'

'His name is Beecham,' St Osyth replied. 'Do you know him?'

'Beecham?' Eugenie repeated doubtfully. 'No, I don't know this name. But he looked at me so particularly. I did not like it at all.'

'I shouldn't let it trouble you, ma'am,' said St Osyth shortly. 'His bad manners are consonant with the rest of his behaviour. He is not received in the best houses, and it is unlikely you will ever be exposed to his insolence again. Unfortunately, my cousin and I are acquainted with him – no more – and must return his bow when in public. But there is no reason for you to notice him at all.'

Eugenie frowned. She had the feeling she had seen him before, but she could not think where, and she was finally forced to conclude that he merely reminded her of someone she knew, for she had been in England for so little time that she would surely remember if she *had* seen him somewhere. She disliked the look of him instinctively, but the Earl's assurance that he was not received was enough to make her dismiss him from her mind. They parted company immediately afterwards, the Earl riding off to join some friends who had called to him, and Sebastian taking up the reins again and nodding to Buckland to take his seat behind, as he had got down and gone to the chestnuts' heads as soon as the Guisborough barouche arrived.

'Well, a pleasant little interlude, don't you think?' Sebastian enquired cheerfully as they moved off. 'You mustn't worry, by the by, if I tilt at Max a little. We are on the best of terms, really. It was dashed good of him to offer us horses for our little expedition to Richmond Park. We must settle a date, and then I'll speak to some other friends of mine about making up a party. These things are nothing without numbers, you know.'

'Had you not better consult with Lord St Osyth before deciding a date?' Eugenie said mildly.

'Oh lord, Max won't be coming with us! This will be an outing for young people, ma'am,' Sebastian said. 'I mean us to enjoy ourselves. We shall have a good gallop, and perhaps a meal *al fresco*, if that suits your ideas. If the weather is good, we can spend the whole day there.'

Eugenie had nothing further to say in opposition, and with an inward smile observed that she was to be the Honourable Sebastian's property in future, if he had anything to say to the matter. St Osyth, however, at two-and-thirty, was considered already to be past enjoying himself, and fit for nothing but marriage to Lady Caroline Stanley.

The Earl was perfectly well aware of what his cousin was up to. The suspicion that Lady Mary might be intending to leave her fortune to Eugenie was enough to make Sebastian anxious to attach himself to her, if possible; and at least by his presence to prevent anyone else doing so. For the rest, his mocking assertions that Lady Guisborough would have her way over the marriage were intended, of course, to point out to St Osyth how objectionable she would be as a mother-in-law, and thereby to give the Earl such a dislike to her that he would avoid the match at all costs. Sebastian was just clever enough to devise this plan, rather than instigate a campaign of direct opposition; and just stupid enough not to know that St Osyth would see through it, or that there was, in fact, no danger of his marrying Caroline Stanley.

From his own observations, he had no doubt that Eugenie was not in the least interested in Sebastian, and that, in fact, her judgement of him coincided closely with St Osyth's own. Though he did not wish to admit it to himself, he was attracted to her, and had they not got off on the wrong foot, through what he considered was no fault of his own, he considered he might even have been in some danger from her: she was intelligent, quick-witted and resourceful, the very opposite from the usual empty-headed females he had had thrust at him by ambitious mamas ever since he left school. There was no doubt, however, that amongst her virtues she also had the very grave faults of being unreasonable, stubborn and pig-headed, and that being so, he had no intention of ever giving her what she wanted: an apology for having splashed her with his curricle on the Kingston road. That he determined against absolutely. But he was piqued enough by her pretended preference for Sebastian to want to shake her a little, to want to make her fall in love with him, just a little, just a salutary amount.

To this end, he set himself to be charming towards her, and began very subtly to woo her. It was an interesting challenge, something to occupy his mind and his resources, for it must be subtle indeed if she were not to suspect him of the very purpose he had in mind. Also, there must be no danger of anyone else's noticing what he was about, for it would not do at all for people to begin talking about them. It would be cruel and quite improper of him to raise her expectations by showing too marked a preference for her; and he would not accord Sebastian the honour of allowing him to think he had a rival. No, he simply wished Eugenie to show him the same degree of calm, friendly preference she now accorded Sebastian, and to smile at him with her eyes as well as her lips.

He didn't think it would be hard to do. She was an intelligent young woman, alone and almost friendless in an alien world, and as such must be grateful for the delicate attentions of someone she could respect. Just as she must know herself far above Sebastian, she would recognise St Osyth as her equal or superior. He would attack her where she was most vulnerable: he would offer her friendship and intelligent conversation. He had already begun his campaign by offering to mount her for her expedition to Richmond Park – an expedition he intended to join, whatever Sebastian thought about it – and he determined to continue the attack at the dress ball to be held at Chelmsford House in Pall Mall on the following evening. He would ask her to dance with him, and in the course of their two dances entertain her so thoroughly that she would consider the rest of the evening flat by comparison. Sebastian would attempt to monopolise her company, of course, but St Osyth was more than equal to vanquishing Sebastian, if it proved necessary. It would be with the senior, and not the junior cousin that Eugenie went in to supper, of that there was no doubt in the world.

Chapter Seven

Eugenie's situation with regard to Lady Mary was a delicate one, for while her ladyship had decided of her own free will to offer Eugenie a home and take the whole expense of her upkeep upon herself, Eugenie could not help feeling a little tender on that score, and endeavoured to limit the expense as far as possible. Lady Mary naturally wished Eugenie to be creditably turned out, and anything of the shoddy or makeshift about Eugenie's appearance she would not tolerate for a moment. Both Eugenie and Marie had such skill with the needle, however, that Lady Mary was forced to admit that even a made-over gown came up as fresh and smart as anything she could have got new from a mantuamaker.

She therefore allowed Eugenie to adapt several old gowns of hers for common use, including a handsome riding habit which had been carefully put away these twenty years, ever since Lady Mary felt herself too matronly to mount a horse. While the style of it was hopelessly outmoded, the cloth was as good as new, and since Lady Mary even in her younger days had been taller and stouter than Eugenie, there proved enough cloth in the habit after unpicking to allow for even the modern long-skirted style.

All the made-over gowns needed fresh trimming, of course, and since some new gowns were also required, for which both material and trimming must be purchased,

Eugenie and Marie spent a great many mornings in the various linendrapers' establishments, such as Harding and Howell's in Pall Mall, Grafton House, and Crook and Besford's. These establishments were much patronised by the wealthier inhabitants of London, and it was frequently necessary to wait as much as half an hour before one could be served. Eugenie took to going out early in order to arrive before the shops grew crowded, and so managed to make her purchases in reasonable comfort.

She was coming out of Grafton House one morning, well pleased with having bought some very pretty edging lace at less than the usual price, as it was from the end of the card, when a touch on her arm arrested her and she turned to find Mr McKendrick beside her, lifting his hat and smiling as broadly as his natural reserve allowed. She greeted him with great pleasure. She had not forgotten her first English friends, and had written several letters to Amabel since arriving in London. Her first enquiry was after Amabel's health.

'Oh, she goes on tolerably well, though somewhat troubled by the sickness in the mornings. But Dacres assures us that the condition is temporary, and that in a week or two it should have passed off.'

'I am very glad to hear it,' Eugenie said, 'for as Mrs McKendrick has not replied to my letters, I feared that perhaps she was too unwell to write to me.'

McKendrick looked a little put out. 'I assure you, ma'am, that Amabel did not mean to neglect you, but she was unsure how you might be placed with Lady Mary with regard to receiving letters. She did not want to make any awkwardness for you, if Lady Mary should object to paying for your correspondence.'

'Ah, that was thoughtful of her,' Eugenie cried.

'In fact, I have about me a letter from her,' he went on, 'and I was intending to do myself the honour of calling on you this morning to deliver it. I had to come to London on business, you see, and Amabel would not miss the opportunity.'

'I am walking back to Brook Street now. Perhaps you would care to walk along with me,' Eugenie said, 'so that we may have a comfortable chat together.'

McKendrick bowed his consent, and then, a little hesitantly, offered his arm, which Eugenie took gladly. His manner might be rather stiff and formal, but it concealed, she was sure, a genuinely kind heart.

'I am glad to have an opportunity of speaking to you privately,' he said as they walked along the crowded flagway, 'for I have some news for you. I have managed to find the inn where you spent your first night in England – '

'My pearls!' Eugenie interrupted in excitement. McKendrick smiled a little.

'Yes, ma'am, indeed. For a wonder, the landlady of the inn had not sold them. I think, perhaps, she may be almost an honest woman.'

'Almost?'

'She says she is quite willing to part from the pearls, but the amount she is asking by way of redemption is much greater than the amount you received from her.'

'Oh!'

'She says – and I suppose that there is some truth in it – that the money she gave you, when you needed it so badly, was worth a great deal more than any amount you may give now, when you have plenty.'

'That's just the thing,' Eugenie said ruefully. 'I have no money. Lady Mary is everything that is generous, and houses, feeds and clothes me, but I have no actual cash, other than what she gives me for my day-to-day needs.'

'I see. And naturally, you would feel delicate about asking her for anything.'

'Naturally.' She thought for a moment, and then sighed. 'I cannot see any way out of it, unless you would do me the kindness of asking the woman to keep the pearls by her until such time in the future as I may be able to redeem them. My servants may still reach England with my belongings, or – or something else may happen, I cannot tell what – but there must come a day when I shall have money at my disposal.' She glanced at him, embarrassed, but he nodded calmly.

'There must indeed, ma'am, for if all else fails, you will one day be married. I fear that the woman's honesty may be stretched a little too far by asking her to wait for such an indefinite period, but I will certainly do my best for you to persuade her.'

'You are very kind,' Eugenie began, but broke off short with a little cry, quickly stifled, as something caught her eye.

'What is it?' McKendrick asked in quick concern.

'Oh, it is nothing, nothing at all. I am being foolish. But I just saw someone – over there, you see, that very dark, swarthy man – there, he is just turning down that alleyway!'

'Yes, I see him. But what of it?'

'It is foolish, as I said, but he was staring at me again. I must have noticed him out of the corner of my eye, for I have the impression he was keeping pace with us on the other side of the road, and watching me.'

'But who is he?' McKendrick asked. 'Why does he alarm you?'

'I don't know. I have seen him staring at me in that way once or twice before, and it upsets me. When I first noticed him, I had the feeling that I knew him from somewhere, but that is absurd, of course. Lord St Osyth says that he is a man, not quite respectable, who lives on the fringes of good society, but that he is not received in the best houses. The Earl has a nodding acquaintance with him. His name is Lambert Beecham.'

McKendrick nodded. 'If you would like me to, I will make some enquiries about him for you – discreetly, of course. His staring at you might be nothing more than impertinence, but if he has some other reason, it will soon become apparent. If his character is doubtful, he may be known amongst the criminal fraternity, which will mean that my legal brethren will certainly know something of him.'

'Thank you,' Eugenie said heartfeltly, 'it would relieve my mind greatly to know what interest he has in me. He troubles me, for what reason I cannot think. But you will not let my name appear in your enquiries?'

'Of course not. Don't be afraid, ma'am, I shall be discretion itself.'

'I'm sure you will. Thank you, Mr McKendrick. You are a true friend.' And she offered him her hand, and when he took it, shook his warmly.

A spell of uncertain weather, and the lameness of a horse, had put off the proposed visit to Richmond Park, but as Town filled up and the Season got properly under way, the weather grew bright and settled, and the proposal was put forward again, with a definite date fixed on. No other delays arose, and on the morning in question, they met at the Roehampton Gate in good time. Apart from Eugenie, Mr Freed and the Earl, the party consisted only of Viscount Scawton and his eldest sister, Lady Caroline Stanley. The reason for this soon became apparent. Mr Freed had invited Scawton as his best friend, and when Scawton had mentioned the matter at home, his mama had insisted that he take Caroline along.

'The Earl will expect it,' she had said confidently, and when Freddy had made so bold as to demur, she had added firmly, 'and if he don't expect it, all the more reason to throw them together. It's more than time he declared himself. If things go on in this way, he'll be making a laughing stock of us. I won't have it. Caroline shall go. She has that crimson habit with the hussar frogging which St Osyth hasn't seen yet. It will make a great impression on him.'

Viscount Freddy had no doubt that it would, but he

wouldn't go so far as to say what impression. The habit was nearer to cherry red than crimson, but neither colour did anything for his sister's sallow complexion and mousy hair, while the high collar and the frogging emphasised her ample bosom until she resembled a bolster. There was no use, however, in arguing with his mother, as he had learnt long ago, and so he informed his friend Sebastian, a little sheepishly, that he would be bringing Caroline with him.

Sebastian was delighted, and refrained from enlarging the party with any more invitations. He reasoned that St Osyth would be forced by mere politeness to ride with Lady Caroline, which would leave his, Sebastian's, way clear with Eugenie. He told Freddy that he was happy to accept the addition to the party, but managed to avoid mentioning it to St Osyth, so that the first he knew about it was when they all met at the gate, by which time it was too late to do anything about it.

St Osyth was mounted on his good bay again, and his groom had brought along a handsome black gelding for Eugenie to ride.

'He may be a little skittish just at first, but there is no vice in him,' he told her. 'It is only playfulness, and if you are an experienced rider, as you indicated you were, you will soon master him.'

'Indeed, I am not the least afraid,' Eugenie said with a smile. 'He is the loveliest creature, and I shall greatly enjoy riding him. My darling Noisette was very playful in just the same way, and I was quite accustomed to her little pranks. I shall have no trouble, I am sure.'

Buckland held the black's head, while St Osyth threw her into the saddle and saw her settled. The horse flinched as the cold saddle pressed on his back and he sidled a little, but after a moment or two he stood still, and St Osyth, watching critically, observed how calm and relaxed Eugenie appeared, how she managed her reins and patted the black neck soothingly, and was satisfied.

'Take him gently at first,' he advised. 'We'll have a canter later to shake the fidgets out of their feet, but you had best walk him quietly with the others to begin with.'

'Thank you, my lord, but I am well in command now. You need not worry about me. I think Lady Caroline is requiring your assistance, is she not?' she added mischievously. St Osyth frowned, but could not, in courtesy, ignore the pointed looks of Lady Caroline and her brother, and was forced to walk over to help her mount. Lady Caroline was an indifferent rider, and her horse was a brown mare with no spirit and no paces, a veritable slug who would never do anything to surprise or unseat her mistress. Viscount Scawton, on the contrary, fancied himself a dashing rider, and added considerably to his father's burdens by going through a procession of flashy, overheated, underboned creatures which usually broke down under his hard riding and had to be sold at a loss. The horse he was attempting to mount at the moment was a rat-tailed, shallow-footed chestnut with a white and rolling eye, which seemed set to break either its own legs or the Viscount's neck. Though it had only been led quietly to the gate that morning by Langton, the Viscount's groom, its coat was already dark with sweat, and it slithered about as Freddy tried to mount, jerking its head up and down in an attempt to free itself and spattering Langton and itself with foam.

Sebastian, already up on his sensible grey, called out to his friend, 'What a fire-eater you have there, Freddy! It's new, ain't it? Where did you get it?'

'Onslow sold it to me,' the Viscount replied as well as he could through his breathlessness, for he was still hopping about with one foot in the stirrup as the chestnut thrashed its quarters this way and that. Buckland caught his master's eye, and went across to take the Viscount's leg and throw him up, lest they be there all day. 'Got it for a good price, too,' he went on as he found his stirrups and gathered the reins. 'Onslow wanted three hundred for it, but I beat him down to two-fifty.'

'That was at least two hundred too much,' said St Osyth drily. 'If I don't mistake, that's the hunter Onslow bought last winter. He only took it out twice – the second time it almost killed him. His groom was for shooting it, but Onslow said he'd run it off for six months and then sell it to some – to someone for a hack.' At the last moment he amended the sentence, for what Onslow had actually said was 'to some fool with more money than sense'.

Scawton did not look at all put out. 'Oh no, St Osyth, you have it wrong, I'm sure. This ain't the same horse. You've only to look at it to see its quality.'

'Yes, I can see its quality very clearly,' said St Osyth drily, and Eugenie suppressed a snort of laughter which drew his eyes to her momentarily. Langton let go of the chestnut's head and it began to walk backwards, shaking its head villainously and dripping foam from its mouth in a constant stream. Lady Caroline was roused from her usual silence to protest in a faint voice.

'Oh Freddy, do be careful. Are you sure it's safe?'

'Of course it is. Don't be a fool, Caro!' Scawton cried crossly. 'Do you think I can't manage my own horse?' And by digging in his spurs, he managed to force the chestnut to relinquish its backward motion in favour of a crab-like progression forwards and sideways. 'Come on then, everyone,' Scawton called cheerfully, seeing that he had got his horse to move in more or less the right direction, 'keep up, can't you?'

The rest of the party set off after him, Lady Caroline's mount being sent forward by a helpful slap on the rump from her groom. The mare had only two paces, walk and halt, but she was not stubborn about it. Once set going, she would go on quietly until told to stop. Eugenie's eyes were dancing with amusement over the difference between the mounts of the brother and sister, and the Earl came up alongside her to remonstrate with her.

'I must beg you not to try to make me laugh,' he said. 'It is too bad of you to make fun of people of fashion.'

'Oh, but no one noticed except you,' Eugenie murmured, 'and really they are too ridiculous.' She clapped her hand over her mouth in a parody of dismay. 'But what am I saying? I do beg your pardon, Earl! I did not mean to insult your future family.'

'That's enough,' St Osyth said firmly. 'You may make fun of anyone except me.'

'Especially when I riding your horse,' Eugenie said demurely. 'And indeed, he is a lovely horse. May we gallop here? Mr Freed says it is not the done thing to gallop in Hyde Park.'

'Yes, it is permitted. We shall gallop in a little while, when the horses have settled down.'

'I do not think the chestnut of Lord Scawton will ever settle until someone puts a bullet through its head,' Eugenie observed judiciously, and St Osyth, feeling his lips tremble, left her side and held back to take his place politely beside Lady Caroline.

Sebastian had only been waiting for this, and quickly took the Earl's place. 'How do you like Blackbird?' he asked Eugenie. 'I've ridden him myself a few times. His paces are pleasant, aren't they?'

'Oh yes; and what a pretty place this is,' she replied agreeably.

'When you get right into the middle of the park, you would think you were in the depth of the country,' Sebastian told her. 'You would never think you were so close to London. It would be quite possible to get lost in here, if you strayed far from the path.'

'I think Lord Scawton is having an uncomfortable ride. I hope he does not stray any further, for he goes much more sideways than forward.'

'Oh Freddy's all right. He's a capital rider, and he'll soon master the brute. Don't you believe what Max was saying about the horse. He thinks he's the only person on the world who knows anything about horseflesh, but Freddy's got a shrewd eye for a bargain. He's a fly one all right. I dare say that chestnut's worth twice what he paid for it. Shall we have a canter now?'

'I think we had better wait a little, until Lord Scawton has a better hold on his horse,' Eugenie said cautiously.

'Oh stuff! Freddy's as right as a trivet. What's the point of coming all this way if we crawl along as if we were in Hyde Park? A canter will be the very thing to quiet the animals down.'

Eugenie was about to argue further with him when the chestnut, whose sideways motion had taken it off the tan into the bracken, disturbed a partridge from the undergrowth. The bird shot across the path right in front of Eugenie's horse. The black snorted in alarm and leapt forward into a canter, and with a whoop of excitement Sebastian took the opportunity to spur his horse forward and gallop after her.

Eugenie was not unseated, and could have stopped the black easily enough had not Sebastian been right behind her urging them both on and making the two horses race each other. She took short pulls at the reins to slow her mount so that Sebastian's grey would outstrip her, and once he had passed, she began to pull up. But before she could complete the action, there was a pounding of hooves behind her, and a glance over her shoulder showed her the Earl galloping towards her flat out, his face grim and angry. In a moment he had come up alongside her, grabbed the reins, and was hauling at both the horses to stop them.

'Let go!' Eugenie cried. 'I have him, I have him!' But St Osyth did not let go. His horse stopped, snorting, in a series of bounces, and the black, pulled off balance, stumbled. His hooves slipping on the dry turf, he kept his feet only by a great lurch which flung Eugenie from the saddle.

She fell into the bracken, and since the horse was almost at a standstill when she parted company with it, she was not hurt, only a little shaken and breathless. But as she sat there panting, watching St Osyth jump from the saddle and fling the reins to the grooms who had just ridden up, she was seething with fury. When he reached her and held out his hand to help her to her feet, she ignored it, and scrambled up by herself, crying:

'That was stupid, stupid! What were you trying to do? You might have hurt me badly, to say nothing of the horse!'

St Osyth's face was as white as hers, his lips a thin line, his nostrils flaring. 'I was about to ask you the same thing,' he said grimly. 'How dare you disobey me? I told you we would walk the horses until they were settled, but you had to have your own way, didn't you? You were so busy thinking you knew better than me, you didn't even consider the danger to others. To gallop off like that without warning was more than stupid, it was irresponsible! Apart from your own neck, you risked Lady Caroline's, to say nothing of the horses' legs, all for your own selfish pleasure!'

'How dare you speak to me like that!' Eugenie cried, stung at the injustice. 'Do you think I galloped off for pleasure? And why did you interfere with my horse? You almost brought him down, grabbing the reins like that.'

'I had to stop him, since you seemed incapable of it.'

'I was stopping him,' she cried furiously. 'I had him well under control when you came rushing up behind. It was thanks to your interference that I came off. I might have been hurt.'

'You should have thought of that before you disobeyed my orders. And if you were as good a horsewoman as you claimed to be, you would not have fallen off, would you?'

'I did not fall off, I was thrown. And once and for all, I did not gallop off for pleasure. My horse was startled by a bird.'

'I saw no bird,' St Osyth said.

'But you must have,' Eugenie said. 'It flew out right under his feet and startled him.' She glared at him, seeing he did not believe her. 'Do you think I am lying about it? Oh, you are impossible!'

'And so are you, madam. I would not have lent you this horse if you had not assured me you were a good horsewoman. To pretend to be better than you are is pitiful. If I'd known, I'd have brought up a quiet hack for you, like Lady Caroline's. That would have been closer to your needs.'

'Oh!' cried Eugenie, so beside herself with fury that she did not consider that St Osyth's rage was far too great for the offence, or that in normal circumstances he would never have spoken so rudely to any lady. They had been so busy shouting at each other, that they had not had time to notice the rest of the party, until Sebastian called to them. He had managed to stop his horse some distance further up the track, and now he had ridden back, and on reaching them he cried out, 'I say, where's Freddy?'

They looked around them. There was Lady Caroline, sitting on her brown mare, and there were the three grooms, Buckland holding the black as well as his own hack, but of Viscount Scawton there was no sign.

'Dash it,' said Sebastian, standing in his stirrups to look round, 'he's gone! That dashed nag of his must have taken off with him into the bracken when he put up that partridge.' St Osyth gave Eugenie a startled glance at the words, but she refused to meet his eyes, her lips still thin with anger. 'I say,' Sebastian went on admiringly to Eugenie, 'you sat your horse like a regular centaur, ma'am! I hope you ain't bruised? Shouldn't have come off – can't think how it happened. You're a dashed fine rider, and plucky! But why did you pull up so soon? We might have had a splendid gallop.'

Eugenie gave him a tight smile, and picking up the skirt of her habit, she tramped back through the bracken to take the reins of the black. Buckland threw her up, and met her eyes with a sympathetic look as she settled herself in the saddle.

'We'd better look for Scawton, I suppose,' St Osyth was saying meanwhile. 'That mad animal's not to be trusted. It might run for ever, or it might come down and break its legs. If Scawton's come to grief, he'll need help. You ladies had better ride back to the gate with Lady Caroline's groom. We'll need Buckland and Langton to help us search. I'm sorry our ride should be so curtailed, but we can come another day.'

'Nonsense,' said Eugenie shortly. 'We will help you search. And it is too soon to be calling off our ride, surely, when for all we know, Viscount Scawton might be making his way back to us at this moment, or perhaps might be waiting for us at the gate.'

'True,' cried Sebastian. 'It would be too dismal for them to be sent home now, Max! We haven't begun to enjoy ourselves.'

'I'm sorry,' said the Earl in a gentle voice, his eyes on Eugenie. 'It may seem dictatorial to you, but that chestnut of Scawton's is dangerous, and even if he were to appear at this moment, I would not consider allowing the ladies to continue riding in its company. I beg you will forgive me, but I must insist that I have my way.'

Eugenie met his eyes in fury and was about to protest, when she saw how earnestly his look begged her not to argue. She swallowed her rage, and smiled with difficulty at Lady Caroline. 'I suppose he is right, ma'am. We had better go back. We shall only be in the way.'

'Poor Freddy, I hope he is all right,' Lady Caroline said. 'Papa was not above half pleased when he bought that horse. But then he never is. Freddy has so many horses, and he never keeps one more than half a year.'

Her groom turned her horse for her and pointed it towards the gate, and St Osyth took the opportunity to edge alongside Eugenie and say in a low voice, 'Thank you. I am sorry your ride should be spoiled, but I am very concerned about Scawton.' She made no reply but a slight bow of the head, and biting his lips, he went on, 'I beg you will forgive my rudeness just then. It was caused only by anxiety for you. I have, I'm afraid, a lamentable temper.'

She looked at him coldly. 'You have indeed, my lord. But you did not seem at all anxious to me, only angry that your orders had been disobeyed. Do not concern yourself, however. Your rudeness did not in any way affect me. It is all just your natural behaviour, I am sure.'

He looked pained. 'Ah!' he said ruefully. 'Now you are in the wrong.' She would not smile, but looked stonily past his left ear. He regarded her for a moment, and then held out his hand and said gently, 'Will you not forgive me? Come, shake hands!'

She met his eyes reluctantly, and saw in them such a mixture of remorse and kindness and amusement and self-mockery that it took her off her guard. Slowly she held out her own hand, and he took it and squeezed her fingers quickly. 'Thank you,' he said. 'God bless you!'

Then calling to the grooms, he led the way into the bracken in search of the Viscount, while Eugenie turned the black and trotted after Lady Caroline and her groom. She was not entirely pleased with herself for having forgiven him. His rudeness and arrogance had been extreme, and his apology inadequate, considering he had almost called her a liar; and he had still never apologised for his first sin towards her on the Kingston road. She was not convinced that he had spoken the truth when he said that his anger was caused by anxiety for her safety, although it had certainly been an inexplicably extreme reaction even from a quick-tempered man. But if he really had felt such concern for her, then surely it must be attributable to a growing *tendresse* for her. There had been that in his eyes, and in his voice when he said, 'God bless you!', which supported the notion.

It would be very good sport, she thought, if she were to make him fall in love with her! Oh, not enough to cause any real damage – and indeed, she was sure that, in his pride, he would never think of her seriously enough to wound him deeply – but enough to puncture his odious arrogance and self-consequence. It would do him a great deal of good, she told herself firmly, to find himself in love and unsure of a return, so pursued and courted as he must have been all his life. Only look at how he treated Lady Caroline! How certain he was that he could marry her if he chose, not considering how she might feel about it.

With a pleasing picture of revenge for the female sex in her head, she caught up with her ladyship, and engaged her in cheerful conversation all the way to the gate.

Chapter Eight

On the morning after the ride in Richmond Park, Lord St Osyth called at Brook Street while the ladies were still sitting in the breakfast parlour to bring news of Viscount Scawton. His horse had bolted with him into a thick tangle of trees and bushes, and, the undergrowth slowing its progress, the worst that might have happened had been avoided. The Viscount was suffering from a broken head, owing to his having involuntarily parted company with the chestnut when it ran under a low branch, and several bruises consequent upon his abrupt descent to the ground. The horse had been halted when its bridle caught in a thicket, and it had sustained nothing worse than a few scratches.

'I called at Stanley House this morning,' St Osyth went on. 'The Viscount was still asleep, the doctor having given him a draught last night to ensure that he had proper rest, but Lord Guisborough assured me that no complications were anticipated. He should be allowed up in a day or two.'

'That is good to hear,' Eugenie said. 'It might have been very bad.'

'Indeed it might,' Lady Mary said tranquilly. 'I was in the greatest anxiety yesterday when Eugenie arrived home so early and told me about it. I sent a note round to Lady Guisborough at once to express my sympathy.'

'Ah yes,' said the Earl, 'she asked me to bring you her

apologies for not having replied to your note yet. She has been too much occupied until now, but assures you she will write later today.'

Lady Mary nodded serenely. 'You have done just as you ought, St Osyth. No little attention ought to be spared in the case of a family with whom you have such particular connections. And it was good of you to bring us the news so quickly, and make us comfortable again.'

'But what of the horse, my lord?' Eugenie asked. 'What will happen to it now?'

'It is to be sold,' said the Earl.

Eugenie raised her brows. 'But who can be found to buy it?'

'Oh, someone will,' he said indifferently.

Eugenie was perturbed. 'But surely no one would buy a horse with such a bad character? And surely Lord Guisborough would not sell it without mentioning its vice? That would be to endanger someone else's life.'

St Osyth was looking uncomfortable, and Lady Mary intervened, saying, 'Depend upon it, my dear, the gentlemen know what they are about. We do not pretend to understand these things. The buying and selling of horses must always remain a mystery to females. My dear Sir Arthur used to buy my carriage horses, and since his death my nephew has done it for me. I have never been able to tell one from another, but Max understands it all. I am sure there is not a man who understands horses better.'

Eugenie was forced to relinquish the subject, though a slight frown between her brows showed that she was not entirely convinced that someone somewhere was not going to be tricked into buying a dangerous horse; and St Osyth's refusal to meet her eye convinced her that he did not condemn the trickery. Lady Mary now introduced the subject of the charity ball at Carlisle House, to which they were going that evening.

'I wonder if the Guisboroughs will care to go, with

young Scawton still abed. Did Lady Guisborough happen to mention it this morning, St Osyth? She must be extremely anxious about the young man; but with three daughters out, she will hardly wish to miss so public an occasion.'

'Lady Guisborough did mention it, ma'am,' said St Osyth. 'She said that they would certainly go, if Scawton was still going on well after dinner. I cannot imagine they will be absent.'

'Oh, then you must certainly ask Lady Caroline for the first two dances. It will be expected.'

'I beg your pardon ma'am,' said St Osyth with a bow towards his aunt and a smile towards Eugenie, 'but Lady Eugenie has already honoured me with her acceptance of my hand for the first two dances. I have been engaged for them these two days.'

Eugenie coloured, and this fresh evidence of his arrogance might have spurred her to expose him, had not she caught his eye at that moment and seen in it a plea of desperation. So it was, when Lady Mary looked towards her in surprise and said, 'Is it true, Eugenie? I wonder you did not mention it to me,' she stammered an excuse and said that it had slipped her mind. Lady Mary looked from one to the other with a thoughtful frown, and a new idea which came to her at that moment was not entirely unwelcome, though she did not yet give up her pet scheme of a match between her nephew and Lady Caroline Stanley. But it was important above all that Max should marry, and if he was beginning to be fond of Eugenie, that might answer almost as well.

The butler entering at that moment with a note which had come round by hand and which needed a reply, Lady Mary was obliged to withdraw to the adjoining morning room. Though she could be seen through the folded back doors, she was far enough away for St Osyth to step close to Eugenie and press her hand and say in a low voice:

'Thank you, from the bottom of my heart. It was like you to be too generous to expose me!'

'That is very well, my lord,' she said severely, 'but now you know we shall have to dance together, and what will you say to that?'

'My dear ma'am, I assure you that nothing will please me more. Does it displease you so much? If so, I shall withdraw from the engagement at once, however much I am embarrassed. But before you speak,' he went on hastily as she opened her mouth to reply, 'I must tell you that part of my purpose in coming here this morning was to secure your hand for those very dances. Lady Mary anticipated me, that was all.'

'Oh, that is neatly done, *par bleu*! You think you have spiked my guns now, don't you, my lord? You think now that I cannot withdraw without either calling you a liar, or appearing ungracious. Well, I shall call your bluff! I shall tell you that I am delighted to be sure of dancing with you, and by no means will I release you from your engagement.'

St Osyth laughed aloud. 'I love the way you eye me sideways like a little bird, and peck at me so fiercely! But indeed, indeed it is true! Please believe me that I came here to ask you to dance.'

'Then you have asked me, and I have accepted. There is no need to make a fuss,' Eugenie said genially. 'Only your poor aunt will be disappointed if you do not dance also with Lady Caroline. She has her heart set upon it.'

'I am glad to see that the hardships you have endured have not driven the wickedness out of you, ma'am,' said St Osyth. 'You may assure yourself, since you seem to take such an interest in my future, that I shall choose my own wife when the time comes.'

Eugenie smiled sweetly. 'I have no doubt about that, my lord. But if you will accept a word of advice, I would say that it would be as well to inform the lady in question that she has been chosen, *before* the wedding day.'

St Osyth chuckled appreciatively, and was about to return the verbal fire when the butler entered again to announce that a Mr McKendrick was calling on Lady Eugenie.

'Oh, please show him in here, Treese,' Eugenie said. St Osyth removed himself a polite distance and picked up a newspaper, but he was still close enough to hear when McKendrick, having made his bow, said, 'I have made some enquiries, ma'am, about this Lambert Beecham.'

St Osyth raised his head on hearing the name, and catching his eye, Eugenie nodded to him and said 'By all means join us, my lord. The business is not private.'

'Well, ma'am, there is not very much I can tell you. He is, as you would expect, deep in debt on a number of fronts, and keeps out of the King's Bench only by a judicious juggling of finances, paying off a little here and a little there to keep his creditors from filing against him. But more seriously,' McKendrick went on, 'he was almost certainly involved last year in a kidnapping case. There was not enough evidence against him to lead to his being brought to trial, or even publicly accused, but my informants assure me that there is very little doubt that he was intimately involved in the matter.'

'What matter?' St Osyth asked sharply.

'It appears he undertook to kidnap a child, the daughter of a wealthy banker, in return for the payment of a large sum of money.'

'But what happened?' Eugenie asked, her eyes anxious.

'The attempt was foiled by the child's nurse raising the alarm,' McKendrick said. 'It seems that Beecham had asked for half his fee before the event, the rest to be paid when he handed over the child to the principals. When the business did not come off, they asked for their money to be returned, but Beecham claimed that he had had to pay it all out in bribes to members of the household, and would not return it. This made the principals so angry that they were ready to peach on him. That's how I have found out as much as I know.'

'What evidence is there that Beecham is the man?' St Osyth asked.

McKendrick shrugged. 'There is no material evidence, my lord, nothing that would serve to convict him in court. But my informants are usually reliable, and they have no doubt it was he. They described him in great detail. I think there is no mistake.'

'This makes him a more dangerous character than I had supposed,' said St Osyth thoughtfully.

'But why is he interested in me?' Eugenie asked, her hand unconsciously at her throat.

'That I have been unable to discover, ma'am. I shall continue enquiries, of course, but perhaps you may have mistaken?'

'I see him so often, and always he stares at me so,' Eugenie said. 'I confess it frightens me.'

'It should not, ma'am,' said St Osyth gently. 'While you are living in this house, you are quite safe. You are not friendless, alone; you have connections. No man, however criminal his intentions, would be mad enough to attempt to harm you.'

'It's true,' McKendrick said. 'You must not be afraid, ma'am. Besides, we have our eye on him now. As soon as he puts a foot wrong, he'll be taken up. And now, if I might introduce a lighter subject,' McKendrick went on with a bow, 'I have a letter here from Amabel to which she is most anxious to receive an answer.'

He handed it to Eugenie, who, with a glance of apology to St Osyth, opened it and perused the contents. 'I am aware of what it says,' McKendrick said, 'and add my urgings to my wife's. The anniversary of our wedding day is to be marked by us with a dinner party, and we should be deeply honoured if you would consider being our guest of honour. It would mean a great deal to both of us.'

'Oh, but of course I will come, if Lady Mary should have no objection,' Eugenie cried at once. She was aware of St Osyth's eyes upon her, and was sure he would be looking amazed and contemptuous at the country lawyer's presumption, and at her willingness to accept. But she didn't care a jot about that, and keeping her own eyes firmly on McKendrick's face she added, 'I should like of all things to see dear Amabel again. If Lady Mary can spare me, nothing will prevent my coming, I assure you!' The McKendricks might not be people of importance, or even people of fashion, but they had been open-heartedly kind and generous to her when she most needed help, and she would not slight them now that she was comfortably situated. She would not have done so even had the invitation been repugnant to her; but as it was, she was truly eager to see dear Amabel and good old Meg again.

Lady Mary was appealed to, and as she saw at once all the propriety of Eugenie's paying such an attention to her former benefactors, she gave her permission, only stipulating that Eugenie should go to Kingston in her coach and be properly attended. She asked a few questions about the condition of the road, the date, the phase of the moon, and the arrangements for her protégée's comfort and safety on both the outward and the return journey, and being satisfied on these points, had nothing further to add. Eugenie penned a brief letter of acceptance and thanks to Amabel, and McKendrick took his departure.

The Honourable Sebastian's capacity for early rising had been stretched to its limits of late, and it was not until almost dinnertime that he presented himself at Brook Street to impart the same news of the previous day's outcome as Eugenie had already received from his cousin. He had the advantage, however, of having seen Viscount Scawton that day, and had some more detail to add.

'I called in on Freddy just before coming here,' he said, lounging gracefully upon the sofa, 'and lord, what a sport he looks, with his head wound up in a great white bandage! But it was only a scalp wound, it seems, and there's no concussion in the case, so he'll be as right as a trivet in no time. He was fussin' to get up today, only the sawbones told him on no account to move out of his bed. And to tell you the truth, I think he's rather glad to stick to his room and avoid his papa, for Guisborough ain't above half pleased about the horse. He read Freddy the most shockin' sermon about it all, and only refrained from boxin' his ears on account of their being hidden under the bandages, so Freddy says.'

'But the horse – it was not hurt, I understand?'

'Oh no. As to that, Buckland and I managed to get the brute free without breakin' anything. We found it caught fast by the head in a hazel thicket, thrashin' about like an eel. It was a deuced difficult piece of work getting near it, but Buckland's a capital fellow with horses, and we brought it off between us all right. There were a few cuts and bruises, nothing that won't heal in a day or two. But the creature must be written off, and Guisborough can't help rememberin' that it was his two hundred and fifty that paid for the nag in the first place, for of course Freddy couldn't meet the bill out of his allowance, and – '

'What can you mean, sir, written off? You said the horse wasn't hurt.'

'Not physically,' Sebastian said, 'but its nerves are shot to pieces. There's no doin' anything with it. It trembles like a leaf if you so much as go near it, and any attempt to touch it drives it to hysteria. I don't suppose anyone will ever be able to ride it again. Guisborough ought to shoot it, to my mind, but he ain't eager to take a dead loss, and sellin' it for fifty guineas is better than nothing.'

Eugenie was shocked. 'But he cannot sell the horse to someone else in that condition. It would be dangerous. Surely – '

'Oh, don't take on, ma'am,' Sebastian interrupted genially. 'He ain't out to rook some flat. The man who's bought it knows all about it. He's going to run it off for six months or a year, and then try to break it in again from the beginning. And I must say, if anyone can do it, it's Max, for between him and Buckland there's nothing they don't know about horses.'

'Earl St Osyth has bought the horse?' Eugenie said in astonishment. 'But he was here only a short while ago, and he did not mention it.'

'Oh, that's like Max – modest to a fault. Bought the nag out of kindness to Freddy, so that Guisborough wouldn't take it out of him too much. And Guisborough ain't such a warm man, either. Fifty guineas is nothing to Max, but it means something to Guisborough.'

'But how kind,' Eugenie said in astonishment. This did not at all accord with the impression she had gained of the Earl. Sebastian eyed her curiously.

'You sound surprised, ma'am. But Max is kind, the kindest man in the world, only damnably stiff and strait-laced at times, and rather too particular about the family name and so on to suit my notions,' he grinned. 'He's always doing good deeds, and taking on deservin' cases and the like. Aunt Mary don't care to have it mentioned,' he added with a sideways glance. 'She don't like Max mixing with fallen women and foundlings and orphans and reformed criminals – thinks it might corrupt him, I suppose, or maybe she's afraid he'll catch fleas. I don't know. But it doesn't bother him. Once Max has set his mind to something, he won't give it up for anyone, you can be sure.'

'Indeed, I had observed that for myself,' Eugenie said thoughtfully. So much was now explained! The 'schemes' that might shock Lady Grantham were nothing worse than schemes of benevolence! Far from being idle, expensive and selfish, St Osyth expended both his time and his money in doing good to others. She had misjudged him, and felt both embarrassed and guilty about it. Perhaps she ought to apologise to him? Ah, but then there was his arrogance and overbearing self-confidence! She had not misjudged that, at least, as his cousin had just confirmed. She entertained herself with wondering whether some of the recipients of his benevolence might be forced to accept it against their will, for she could imagine that when St Osyth had decided to do someone good, they would be done good to, whether they liked it or not! But justice where it was due: he was a much better man than she had supposed, and her future dealings with him must be modified accordingly. If he could only be brought to acknowledge his faults and make a suitable apology to her, she might even feel herself at liberty to like him very well.

Since arriving in London, Eugenie's time had been pretty well accounted for in attendance on Lady Mary and in the engagements she had arranged for her. This did not mean that she had forgotten her missing servants, or had given up hope of finding them again. She had not been at liberty to make enquiries for them in person, but whenever she could be spared, Marie, whose English had improved by leaps and bounds to the point where she could safely go out alone, was frequently visiting the village of Brompton where the *émigrés* mostly lived.

It was not a chore to her, for in Brompton she made many friends amongst her fellow countrymen. Though her principal reason for going was to ask for news of Nana and Pierre, she spent many happy hours there chatting in the French language which she sorely missed elsewhere, talking over old times, swapping anecdotes, and making herself useful about the houses of her new friends. She felt more at home with them than she did amongst the servants of Berrington House, whom she felt looked down on her.

Though Eugenie had little money of her own, Marie never went empty-handed if she could help it, and there was usually a shirt Eugenie had sewn, or a basket of scraps she had cozened out of the cook, or a bottle of soothing syrup for someone's cough. Marie brought back messages of thanks, a glow of happiness, and interesting items of news that could be had nowhere else. On the day of the charity ball, she had been given permission to go to Brompton on condition that she returned in time to help Eugenie dress. She arrived in good time, but ran straight upstairs to her mistress's room in a state of great agitation, without even pausing to take off her outdoor clothes.

Eugenie was in her dressing gown, ready to take her bath, which was being filled for her by a very young housemaid. She jumped up in consternation as Marie came in, seeing how pale she looked, and cried, 'What is it? What has happened? Is someone ill?'

She had instinctively spoken in French, and Marie, with a glance at the housemaid, replied in the same language.

'Oh no, madame, no one is ill, but I have learned something today which is very bad indeed. It is about that man.'

'You mean Beecham?' Eugenie asked.

'The same, madame, but his name is not Beecham. It is *Beauchamp*, only the other is the way the English pronounce it. *Lambert Beauchamp*. He is a Frenchman, madame.'

'Are you sure? How do you know that?'

'He is very well known in Brompton. They all know him there, and hate and fear him. When they told me today who he was I almost fainted! Oh madame, he is an agent of Robespierre!'

Eugenie turned pale. 'It can't be true!'

'But it is, madame! He has been back and forth to France a dozen times in the past year. His special task is to trace certain people in whom Robespierre is interested, and take them back to France to stand trial for what the revolutionaries like to call Crimes Against the People.'

'I understand,' said Eugenie. 'Helping people to escape to England, you mean?'

'Yes, madame, amongst others. He takes them, by force if necessary – '

'It must always be necessary. Anyone who is charged

before the Revolutionary Tribunal inevitably goes to the guillotine. There is no escape. To be taken to France in those circumstances is to be taken to one's death.' She took a turn up and down the room in anxious thought. 'But are you sure it is the same man? Surely it cannot be! The Earl and his cousin both know this man. They are both convinced he is an Englishman, and the Earl, at least, is no fool.'

'Oh he is cunning, this Beauchamp. Before the revolution, he was forced to flee France to escape imprisonment for debt. He spent many years in England, living in London until he was taken for an Englishman, learning to speak English with no accent, making acquaintances amongst the rich who would be of most use to him. But he was soon in debt here, too. When the revolution happened, he thought it was his chance to go home again, and he slipped across to France, but though the government had changed, there were too many there who knew him. He was taken up for debt, but Robespierre had him released on condition that he worked for him.'

'He had no choice, then,' said Eugenie.

'Indeed he had,' Marie said indignantly. 'Once he was back in England, he might have thumbed his nose at the old spider. But as always he needed money, and Robespierre pays him for his dirty work.'

'I thought I recognised him when first I saw him,' Eugenie mused. 'It is quite possible that I had seen him in the background at Versailles or in Paris. One of those people you observe out of the corner of your eye and then forget about.'

'He certainly knows who you are, madame,' said Marie, wringing her hands, 'and worse still, he has been asking questions about you in Brompton. That was how I found out who he is. Madame Maine, who I was visiting today, told me about it so that I could warn you, and I came home as quickly as I could. Oh madame, what are we to do?'

'Peace, Marie, don't panic so. Let me think. Did it emerge from what Madame Maine said that he has a special interest in me? Has he been given orders to capture me and take me back to France, or is he asking only out of curiosity, in case I might be useful to him?'

'I don't know, madame. She didn't say. But you did help your father with his work. And they did try to capture us as we were escaping.'

Eugenie was still thinking. 'I have been in London for some months now, and yet he has done nothing more than stare at me and ask questions. His interest must be idle.'

'I pray so, madame, but I dare not believe it.'

'And as the Earl says, he would not dare to move against me when I am surrounded by wealthy and influential people. I am not alone and unprotected. This Beauchamp cannot suppose he could take me from under the noses of so many people.'

'Oh madame, I beg you to be careful,' Marie moaned. 'There is no knowing what this devil might do. He is dangerous, madame. All our people in Brompton hate and fear him.'

'I shall be careful, Marie, never fear. But I think we should not mention this to Lady Mary. It might frighten her very much, and I should not care to do anything to make her uncomfortable.'

'Very well, madame. But what about his lordship? Will you not tell him? If he knows the truth, he may be able to have this Beauchamp locked up.'

'I don't know about that, Marie. The law in England is a very strange thing. But I think I shall tell him, for if anything were to happen – '

Marie shivered. 'Oh don't speak of it, madame. It is too dreadful.'

It was certainly a very alarming prospect, and Eugenie might be forgiven for starting nervously at every sudden sound, and for looking about her very carefully when she stepped out of the house and crossed the pavement to the waiting carriage which was to take her to the ball that evening. She chided herself, however, for her foolishness, for even if Beauchamp did have the intention of trying to kidnap her, he would scarcely have tried to do so under the noses of Lady Mary, her maid, the coachman, the two footmen who rode behind, the two menservants from the house who were helping them into the carriage, and the butler and porter who were standing in the doorway to see them off – to say nothing of the usual passers-by in the street and all the other carriages passing up and down the road. If she took reasonable care to avoid being alone in strange places, she could not see what he could do against her. Firmly she dismissed the threat from her mind and prepared to enjoy herself.

The ball was a brilliant occasion, and since the proceeds were to go to a hospital which was a very popular charity amongst the great ladies of society, it was certain to be extremely well patronised. It was Lady Mary's habit to arrive early at functions of this sort, in order to secure herself a comfortable place by the fire, but despite her punctuality the rooms were already so crowded that it seemed certain the ball would attract to itself the ultimate accolade of being designated "a sad crush".

'Everyone seems to be here, my dear,' Lady Mary remarked to Eugenie as they passed through the first pair of doors. 'Why, there's old Lady Stokes! I don't believe she has accepted an invitation for eighteen months or more. And Mrs Derminster over there, talking to Sir Humphrey Barstowe – she was a Brandon, you know. They say Carstairs was mad for her before she married Derminster, but it was a love match, and Lord Brandon wouldn't go against her wishes. She gave up society when Derminster died. I think this is the first time I have seen her in public. Dear me,' she added in a pleased voice, 'this really is a most shocking crush! Do take care of your train, my dear. It would be a sad thing if that lace were to be torn.'

They reached a satisfactory position in the main room just before the country dances began, and no sooner were they settled than Lord St Osyth presented himself with a bow to his aunt and a smile for Eugenie, to whom he offered his arm, saying, 'I believe, ma'am, that we are engaged for this dance?'

'Well,' cried Lady Mary, 'For once in your life you are punctual, St Osyth! It does you credit. Yes, go along, my dear, by all means. Enjoy yourself. See, here is dear Lady Guisborough approaching, so I shall not want for company.'

St Osyth, out of his aunt's line of vision, rolled his eyes in mock horror at the last words and hurried Eugenie away towards the forming sets. 'I must thank you from the heart, ma'am, for giving me the means of escape,' he murmured, and Eugenie smiled wickedly.

'A temporary escape only, my lord, for, you know, you must take me back at the end of the dance, and what shall save you then?'

'I shall ask you to dance again,' he said. She opened her eyes wide.

'A second time so soon? And in public? Would you set everyone talking, sir?'

'I think I would almost rather do that than dance with Lady Caroline,' he said. Eugenie looked stern.

'You assume too much, Lord St Osyth. Who is to say that the Lady Caroline will be free? Or that she would accept you if she were?'

'You are quite right. I am properly humbled. May she never lack for partners – especially at any dance where I am present.'

'Pah! You are incorrigible!' Eugenie said. 'However, I also have been guilty of making assumptions, which I find I must now change.'

'About what, ma'am?'

'About you, my lord.' He raised his eyebrows in polite wonder. 'I had thought, you see,' she explained, 'that because you had behaved so unforgivably towards me, that there was no virtue in you. But I find I was wrong.'

'I'm glad to hear it,' he said mildly. 'What have I done to raise your opinion of me?'

'Nothing to me. But you have been kind towards Lord Guisborough, and I am to understand that it is not the only example of your kindness.'

'Ah! My cousin Sebastian has been talking to you, I collect. It is not wise to believe everything he says.'

'I think I can judge what to believe and what not to believe,' Eugenie said. 'You have your faults – grave ones – but your virtues are now known to me also.'

St Osyth laughed. 'I admire your frankness, ma'am, extremely! But I am sorry to know that my behaviour towards you was *unforgivable*. Is there no hope for me? May I never be pardoned?'

'Oh yes,' said Eugenie genially, 'in a moment. There will not be the least difficulty about it. You have only to apologise.'

'Ah,' he said lightly, 'then I must continue to suffer.'

She glared at him and opened her mouth to reply, but her rebuke remained unspoken. Beyond the lines of dancers, seen clearly through a gap between the shoulders of the men and the feathers of the women, she had seen Beauchamp standing by the door as if he had just come in. He was looking about him alertly, and Eugenie seemed to shrink into herself, as if instinctively making herself smaller and less visible. Her partner was not slow to notice the change in her. His mocking smile was replaced with a look of genuine concern.

'What is it?' he asked gently. 'A change has come over you. What have you seen that troubles you?'

'It is that man again. Over there, by the door. He looks for me, but he does not see me yet,' she said almost in a whisper.

St Osyth pressed her hand warmly and said in encouraging tones, 'You mean Beecham? But you must not let him frighten you so! He cannot harm you.'

'He is not Beecham, he is *Beauchamp*. I know all about him now, and he can do me the greatest harm,' Eugenie said, and in quick, low accents she told St Osyth all she had learnt that day. He listened attentively, his face grave, and when she had finished he said:

'Yes, it all accords with what I know of him. I am glad, very glad, that you have trusted me with your confidence. But you must not allow yourself to be overpowered. In all probability he is not here on your account.'

'Then why is he here?'

'It is a public ball, the sort of occasion he would be careful not to miss. There is every reason for him to be here. It may have nothing to do with you.'

Eugenie shivered. 'He is looking for me, I know it.'

He did not argue with her further, only pressed her hand again, and looked warmly into her eyes. 'Very well, it shall be as you say. But you must believe that you are safe with me. He would never dare to move against you while you are under my protection, and I should never let the slightest harm come to you. You must know – ' He broke off abruptly, looking a little confused. Eugenie looked up into his eyes, and felt her cheeks growing warm.

'Yes?' she prompted him, hesitantly.

'You are my aunt's protégée,' he resumed after a moment. 'As head of the family I am responsible for your safety and comfort, as I am for hers.'

'Oh,' said Eugenie, and lowered her eyes. St Osyth looked across her bent head and found himself staring straight at Beauchamp, who for an instant glared at him with an expression of dark and glittering hatred before the gap in the crowd closed again and hid him from view.

Chapter Nine

The Orange Tree in Kingston High Street was noted for its ordinary, and for the numbers of gentlemen of the legal profession who took their midday meal there. The coffee room was provided with a row of convenient booths, furnished with benches and tables, in which gentlemen from the offices of the local attorneys-at-law might sit and take their chop together and discuss business without, unless they forgot themselves and raised their voices too high, being overheard by the gentlemen from the rival firm in the next booth.

Mr Thomas Martin of the firm of Spennilow and McKendrick, whose particular fondness for a certain kind of brown sauce served with the mutton chops had been detected by Eugenie in its effect upon his waistcoats, was to be found in the Orange Tree on most days. Occasionally he was privileged to take his mutton in the company of one of his principals, as on the day after the charity ball. Mr McKendrick smiled upon him almost genially and said that he would walk down to the Orange Tree with him.

'And perhaps we may order a pint of wine with the ordinary, eh, Martin? I have something to celebrate.'

'In that case, sir, I should be happy to accommodate you,' said Martin with a cheerful grin. 'It would be a poor thing to leave a man to celebrate on his own. May I ask the nature of your good news, sir?'

Over the beefsteak, onions and fried cabbage which was that day's ordinary, McKendrick told Martin about the proposed dinner party, and so quickly did the pint of port wine go down that Martin thought it only right to reciprocate with the purchase of another. McKendrick, normally an abstemious man, was unused to drinking such a quantity of wine in the middle of the day, and his voice grew a little louder and his tongue a little looser than was normal. To Martin, his frosty senior suddenly seemed delightfully human, and he encouraged McKendrick's loquacity by his sincere interest in anything to do with Eugenie. McKendrick was too good a lawyer to reveal, even when slightly bosky, anything of the Comtesse's business concerns, and Martin saw no need to attempt to restrain his companion, even had such an attempt been thinkable in a junior employee. When dinner was over and they left their booth to return to the office, Martin saw out of the corner of his eye that the man in the next booth turned his head to give them a quick, comprehensive glance, and supposed that he must have been listening to their conversation this last half-hour; but they had talked of nothing that was confidential, and Martin dismissed it from his mind as unimportant.

He would probably not have thought about the incident again, had not something happened the following evening to draw his attention to it forcibly. He had been out to dinner with his friend 'Stuffy' Wilson, a counting-house clerk who lodged in the same house, and with whom he had in common an unquenchable good humour and a desire to save the experience of their landlady's cooking until the end of the month when money ran low. They had dined at the Orange Tree, and the occasion being Stuffy's birthday, the wine had flowed pretty freely. The heating effect of wine upon the brain of impoverished young clerks is well known, and when they had eaten and drunk themselves hilarious, they staggered out into the warm night air of Kingston, and found in themselves a deep unwillingness to go home to bed. It would be too dashed flat by half.

'You're a capital fellow, Tom!' Stuffy told him earnestly, leaning against his shoulder and breathing vinously into his ear. 'Had a splendid evening. Don't want it to end yet.'

'Lord, no!' said Martin with a gentle hiccough. 'The night's young. What say we have some brandy?'

'Brandy, yes! The very thing! I'm dashed thirsty.'

'Brandy ain't the thing for thirst, old fellow,' Martin told him. 'Your trouble, Stuffy, is that you haven't any brains.'

'True,' said Stuffy amiably. 'Never had any. Just like m'father. Like m'grandfather too. No brains in the whole family. Never mind, s'long as a fellow's got friends like you, Tom! Where are we going now?'

Martin stared owlishly at his feet for a moment or two to concentrate his mind, and then his brow cleared. 'Brandy,' he recollected, and was turning back towards the doors of the Orange Tree when Stuffy said, 'Wait up, old fellow. Not in there. Got a better idea. Let's go to the Dog and Duck!'

'Dog and Duck? What Dog and Duck? Don't know any Dog and Duck.'

'Yes you do, Tom,' Stuffy said earnestly. 'Took you there on *your* birthday. Down in Water Lane. You remember.'

'Oh, that Dog and Duck! Yes, all right, then. We'll go and have some brandy there. They have real French brandy don't they?'

Stuffy leaned so close he almost overbalanced. 'Ssshh!' he hissed, his finger wavering about in search of his lips. 'Not so loud. It's smuggled French brandy, don't forget!'

'Oh yes – forgot. Mum's the word.'

Water Lane was a narrow, dark and muddy street close to the river, one of a labyrinth of lanes winding amongst tumbledown and slatternly houses to a mud foreshore beside the bridge. The Dog and Duck was a dimly lit, smoky and verminous place of ill repute, to which respectable young gentlemen only had recourse when they were on far from respectable business. The ale there was sulphurous and adulterated, but from time to time they had shipments of smuggled and probably stolen brandy and wine, and for the less particular there were young women of doubtful antecedents but great commercial willingness. It was a place where a drunken young gentleman might be reasonably sure of having his pocket picked within the first half-hour, and of coming out with considerably more livestock about his person than when he went in. But Stuffy and Martin had very little money left after their dinner, and meant to have spent it well within the half-hour; portable vermin were one of the accepted hazards of life, and easily dealt with.

The walk down to Water Lane sobered Martin – who was in any case not so drunk as his friend – sufficiently to persuade him that it would be a good idea for both of them to remove anything of value about their persons to their front-breeches pockets, where lifting it would be a job for an amorous young woman's fingers. Having taken this precaution, they plunged down the dark and malodorous alley, through the hospitably open door of the tavern, and into what served it for a coffee room.

The lighting was poor, and the quantity of tobacco smoke, added to the smoke from the fat-burning lamps, made it hard to see across the room. The two young men lurched happily across to the only empty table, which was at the far side, right beside a doorway covered with a heavy and greasy baize curtain, beyond which, they knew, was a tiny private room where there was usually to be found one of the commercial young ladies plying her trade. An idiot in a soiled apron who worked as a waiter limped over to them, and they bellowed 'brandy' at him only two or three times before he grasped the nature of their wishes, grinned, and limped off to fetch them a bottle and two tankards.

'This place,' said Stuffy solemnly, when the bottle had been tilted and a toast drunk, 'is utterly vile.'

136

'Intolerably so,' Martin agreed.

'Ought to be shut down.'

'Without a doubt. Shut down immediately.'

Stuffy lifted his tankard, and after two attempts got it to his lips. 'Splendid brandy, though. Here's to it!'

'Confusion to our enemies!' Martin added, and drank.

It was quite shortly after that that a tall and slatternly young woman came across to them, leaned over the table to display her half-bare breasts, and smiled a semi-toothless smile at them, saying, 'Ullo, boys! 'aving a good time, are we? What say we make a party of it? I got a friend over there'll join us.'

Martin, still fairly sober, managed to suppress his instinctive horror at the idea of what her greasy clothing might conceal, and said with perfect courtesy, 'Sorry, ma'am, we can't oblige you. We've been celebrating, you see, and we've just spent the last of our money on this brandy. We're absolutely penniless now.'

'Pockets to let,' Stuffy added, goggling at her. She sniffed disbelievingly, eyed them like a crow eyeing a well-picked carcase on a hillside, and then straightened up, tossing her head.

'Pox on you then,' she returned civilly, and drew aside the curtain of the private room to see if there was any trade within. Martin, who had turned his head with her, saw the tiny space lighted like a scene upon the stage of a theatre. In the windowless little room – hardly more than a deep alcove – there was a round table with four stools drawn up to it. Seated on three of the stools were three burly men in shabby, nondescript clothing, and on the fourth, his face turned angrily towards the open doorway, was the dark man who had been in the booth next to Martin and McKendrick at the Orange Tree the day before.

'Get out of here!' he told the young woman sharply. 'Drop that curtain, damn you!'

'Oh, sorry I'm sure!' she said, flouncing away, and the curtain fell back into place.

Martin was a quick-witted, noticing sort of young man, and in the instant that the curtain had been drawn aside he had taken in the whole scene, and instinctively drew himself back from the opening so that the dark man would not see him. On the table there had been a lamp, several bottles and cups, and, he was certain, a leather money bag. The dark man had been leaning across the table with one finger raised against the palm of the other hand, as though emphasising an important point he was making. His face was turned towards the door, and the tone of his voice had been furious and menacing, enough to prevent the young woman from even thinking of arguing with him, or pressing her trade. Two of the other three men had had their backs to him, but the one whose face he could see had not been a pretty sight: a brutish, unshaven visage, made horrible by a knife-scar running up one cheek and across the eye socket, in which a white and sightless eye glared out blindly from the puckered lids.

There was no doubt in his mind that the dark man was up to no good, and that the other three were a species of low life that he was hiring for some criminal and probably violent purpose, for they were strong and burly and looked as though there was nothing they wouldn't do for money. The memory of the searching look the dark man had given him and McKendrick as they left their booth in the Orange Tree made him think at once of the comtesse. McKendrick had been talking about her visiting him in Kingston. Was it only a coincidence that the dark man was here, the very next day, apparently hiring criminal accomplices for some nefarious purpose? Or was it that he was on the high toby, and that what was being planned here was highway robbery, with the robbers having the advantage of knowing exactly who was coming, and when, and by what route?

Certainly it was not a possibility he dared dismiss without investigation. A faint line of light down the side of the curtain showed him that, as might be expected in a house like this, the walls were not true, so that the curtain, hanging as it must in accordance with natural laws, did not lie quite against the frame of the door. There was a gap, and where light could pass, so, he imagined, could sound. With infinite care, he edged his chair closer to the doorway, and by leaning back against the wall, he was able to position his ear right by the gap.

It was not easy to overhear anything. For one thing, the dark man was doing most of the talking, and he was on the far side from him, and was speaking, as one would expect, in a low voice. For another, the noise in the coffee room was great, and no inconsiderable portion of it was emanating from Stuffy Wilson, who had reached the musical stage of inebriation. That had the advantage of keeping him entertained, so that he would not immediately miss Martin's conversation, but it took great control of mind to shut out all the other noises in order to concentrate on the dark man's voice.

At first he could only pick out a word here and there, nothing that he could piece together, but then he heard the man nearest him say, 'What about pops, guv'nor? Me and my mates don't reckon to do nothin' o' this sort wivout we got pops along of us.'

The dark man's voice came back clearly, raised a little with urgency. 'There's to be no shooting. Understand that! It's too dangerous. Guns have a habit of going off accidentally, and the wrong person might get hit. She's no use to me dead. She must be taken alive.'

Martin felt as though all the blood in his body had suddenly turned white. Taken alive? Good God, it was not robbery they were after, it was kidnapping! The dark man meant to kidnap Eugenie! Hastily he moved his ear a fraction closer to the gap in the curtain, and strained his attention.

The nearest man was arguing about firearms. 'Don't tell me a swell mort like that ain't going to be travelling wiv guards! And don't tell me the guards ain't going to 'ave arms! I don't aim to get my 'ead blown off, no, not even for your gold, guv'nor, so you can forget it.'

A new voice joined in, very low and hoarse, almost a whisper, but an involuntary one, as though the speaker had sustained damage to his throat. Martin guessed it was the one-eyed man. 'Sides, what's to make 'em stop the kerridge, if we ain't got pops? They'll just ride us down. On'y a fool would stop in Marble Woods just 'cos some cove in a mask asks 'im to!'

'Shut up, you fool!' came the dark man's voice. 'I didn't say you'd have no guns, only that there'll be no shooting. And the carriage will stop all right – I'll see to that. Listen!'

Martin did his best to oblige, but as the dark man lowered his voice at that point, he was once again able to distinguish only the occasional word in the murmur. So hard was he concentrating that it was almost his undoing. The voices had ceased altogether, and it was only the scrape of a stool which warned him in time that the conference was over and the men were coming out. If they guessed he had been listening, he had no doubt that his life would be worth nothing; moreover, the dark man knew his face, and if he recognised him now all hope of warning Eugenie would be lost. With a speed of reaction born of desperation, he whipped his chair back the inches he had stolen, and flung himself face down across the table as though in a drunken stupor. There was no time to do more.

He heard the sounds of the men coming out, the scuffing of feet, the rattle of the curtain rings, the movement of air about him. Stuffy was still singing happily, having noticed nothing of his surroundings since the beginning of his last chorus about the fate of The Pretty Cherry-picker. Martin remained still, trying to breathe slowly and regularly as one would expect of a drunkard, while inside his heart thundered and his bowels loosened with terror. At any moment he expected to feel a hand on his shoulder. He imagined the dark man, cautious and suspicious, lifting up his head by the hair to look at his face. After that there would come the scuffle in the dark, the blow on the back of the head or the knife in the ribs, and his body would go floating anonymously off down the Thames. He strained his ears until his head felt ready to burst. Surely they had not gone? Surely the dark man was standing over him, just waiting for him to move. As soon as he opened an eye, he would pounce.

Through the pounding in his head he heard Stuffy begin another chorus, and then break off, and when he patted his friend on the shoulder Martin almost started out of his skin. 'Tom, you all right, old fellow? You not feelin' quite the thing? Shame to go to sleep here, though. Have some more brandy, that'll make you feel better. Excellent brandy this. Put you on top of the world.'

They had gone. Martin opened an eye, then both, then sat up, and the empty alcove mocked his fears. He was stone sober, and felt an urgent need to be sick. Stuffy beamed at him.

'Havin' a wonderful birthday, Tom dear fellow. Do the same for you next time. Recip-reciprocate, you know. Feelin' wonderful. Not a care in the world.'

An abbreviated and restless night's sleep, with dreams made sinister with dark and threatening faces, followed the excitements of the evening and the overconsumption of heating liquors. Martin woke late the following morning with a headache and a foul taste in his mouth, and a profound depression of mind which resolved itself, as soon as he remembered what had happened, into violent activity.

He flung himself out of bed, washed hastily, shaved himself more than usually at random, flung on his clothes, and hurried off to the offices of Spennilow and McKendrick, where he sought an immediate audience with the junior partner. McKendrick listened to him gravely, and Martin had never liked him so well as when he displayed his instant grasp of the basic facts, without wasting time on disbelief or exclamation.

'It is quite clear what we must do,' McKendrick said at once. 'We must go to the Earl of St Osyth. As head of the family, he is the proper person to inform. We had better go at once. Are you ready to ride to London with me?'

'Yes sir.'

'My horse is at the King's Head. We can hire another there for you. You did quite right to come to me, Martin. This man is dangerous – thank God he did not see you.'

'You know who he is, then, sir?'

'Yes,' said McKendrick grimly. 'From your description I have no doubt it is Lambert Beauchamp.'

The Earl was not at home when the two men presented themselves at his house in Grosvenor Square. His butler advised them that his lordship was out driving the Comtesse de Talcy in the Park, and when they spoke of their business being urgent, he assured them that his lordship would be returning to dress for dinner, and invited them to wait in the business room.

This small room off the main hall was furnished with comfortable leather chairs as well as a large writing desk which the legal gentlemen were sorry to see was covered with a very untidy heap of ledgers and papers, giving the impression that his lordship's business affairs were not being taken care of as they ought. It seemed a long a weary wait, and Martin was conscious of having to restrain his natural impulse to sort out the mess upon the desk. Whoever was the Earl's secretary, he had not been trained in the best traditions.

At last sounds of arrival were heard from the hall, and St Osyth wasted no time in coming to see what they wanted: the door opened almost immediately, and the Earl was seen still stripping off his gloves, which he threw to the waiting footman before dismissing him with a wave of the hand.

'Well, gentlemen, what have you to tell me?' he asked, closing the door behind him.

'My lord, may I present Mr Thomas Martin, who is a confidential clerk in my offices? He has fresh and very important information about the man Beauchamp.' Martin bowed to the Earl, who returned it with a nod and a very sharp look.

'Please sit down, gentlemen. Mr Martin, you have my complete attention.'

Martin gave the Earl a condensed account of his experiences the night before. 'I told Mr McKendrick first thing this morning, my lord, and he believed from my description that the dark man was Beauchamp.'

'I'm sure he is right. But I wonder how he came to be in Kingston,' St Osyth mused. 'Could that have been coincidence? It seems unlikely.'

McKendrick started as a thought came to him. 'My lord – I believe – Yes, of course, he must have seen me talking to her ladyship outside Grafton House! I remember at the time she said she had seen him on the other side of the road, watching us. I did not at that time see him myself, so I forgot about it.'

'Hmm. Perhaps so,' St Osyth said. 'But if he has been watching Berrington House, as he may well have been doing, he must have seen you coming and going. It would not be difficult to find out who you were, or to trace you to Kingston. But how did he know that Lady Eugenie proposes to visit you?'

'Ah, that, I'm afraid, is my fault, my lord. He overheard me telling Martin about it on Tuesday,' McKendrick said wretchedly. 'Martin saw him apparently taking notice. That was what alerted him when he saw the man again last night.'

The Earl was thoughtful. 'There is no need to blame yourself. He might have found that out from one of many sources, and it has, at least, been useful in making him show his hand.'

'You believe, then, that he intends to capture her ladyship and demand ransom for her return?' Martin asked.

'The danger is more acute than that,' St Osyth said. 'We have recently learnt that Beauchamp is an agent of Robespierre. We believe that he has orders to take her ladyship back to France to stand trial for her anti-revolutionary activities. Once she was in Robespierre's hands, her death would be certain.'

The two men nodded gravely, and McKendrick said, 'We must ensure, then, that her ladyship takes no risks. Naturally she must cancel her engagement at my house, and go nowhere without an escort – armed if need be.'

Martin looked appalled. 'For the rest of her life? Such a restriction on her freedom would be intolerable. Surely we must find some way of taking up this Beauchamp and ending the threat once and for all?'

'I don't believe it would be for the rest of her life,' McKendrick said calmly. 'Matters in France are coming to a climax. The atrocious killings in Paris – this 'Great Terror' of theirs – cannot go on indefinitely. Sooner or later sanity will assert itself, Robespierre and his cronies will be overthrown, and the threat to her ladyship will be removed.'

'Sooner or later! – ' Martin began hotly, but the Earl interrupted.

'I agree with you, McKendrick, that Robespierre cannot retain power for ever. But I'm afraid I do not agree with your conclusion that his removal would make her ladyship safe. As long as Beauchamp is at large, she will be in danger from him. There has been a development which alters things. He now knows, you see, that my interest in the Comtesse is more than, shall we say, a friendly one.'

McKendrick and Martin looked at him with interest, and he met their regard blandly. There was a moment's tactful silence as each considered the possibilities. Beauchamp now had a double interest in kidnapping Eugenie, for he could also use her to extort a large ransom from St Osyth, who was in fact as well as by repute one of the wealthiest men in England; and St Osyth also knew that he had a personal reason for wanting to hit at him. He had not forgotten the look of burning hatred he had intercepted from Beauchamp, and how angry he was at the failure of his contrivance over the gold snuffbox. And in the unlikely event that St Osyth refused to pay the ransom to secure the return of Eugenie, the villain could still recoup at least a part of his fortune by selling her to Robespierre.

'Well, then,' Martin said at last, 'the only thing to do is to take him up.'

'More easily said than done,' McKendrick said, shaking his head. 'He has always been very careful to do nothing that would endanger him under the law, and I don't believe your evidence in this matter, Martin, would be sufficient to secure a conviction. If we took him to court and lost, he would be more dangerous than ever.'

'The wounded fox . . .' the Earl murmured.

Martin met the Earl's eye, and had the curious feeling that their thoughts were running as one. 'Perhaps if we encouraged him to go ahead with his plans for the kidnapping . . .' he said slowly, and the Earl gave him a tight smile.

'Yes, my thoughts exactly. If he were caught in the act of attempting to kidnap her ladyship, there could be no doubt about his conviction under the law. What is the penalty for kidnapping, McKendrick?'

'Imprisonment for life, or transportation,' he said absently. 'But we cannot place her ladyship in so much danger. It would be irresponsible.'

'Better that than a lifetime of fear, never knowing where he might strike,' St Osyth said.

For the next two hours the three men discussed plans, and were interrupted at last by the anxious appearance of his lordship's valet, who wished to remind his master that it was past time for him to dress for his dinner engagement.

'Gentlemen, I must leave you. Let us all think over what

we have been saying, and meet again tomorrow morning to discuss it more fully. We can at least be fairly sure now that Beauchamp will not move against her ladyship until the day of her visit to Kingston, and that gives us time to make sure our plans are watertight. I need not remind you, of course, that we must all maintain the strictest secrecy. For the moment, no one but ourselves must know anything of what we have been discussing.'

'And her ladyship, sir?' Martin asked. 'Will you tell her?'

The Earl hesitated. His relationship with Eugenie was in any case at a delicate state, and he could hardly be blamed for not wanting to tell her that his interest in her was actually increasing the danger to her. 'I think not – certainly not for the moment. It is essential that nothing about the behaviour of any of us should change, or the quarry might be frightened off. No, for the moment at least I shall not tell her.'

The two legal gentlemen left to ride back to Kingston, and the Earl followed his man upstairs to be dressed for dinner and the visit to the theatre which was planned for that evening. He had expected it to be an effort to clear his mind of the afternoon's events and to behave as if everything was as normal, but ten minutes in Eugenie's company made the pretence of being relaxed and happy almost a reality. Dressed all in white, she looked exquisitely lovely, and never had her charm and sparkling wit endeared her to him more. In the half-darkness of the theatre, he was able to indulge himself in looking at her without being observed, and his only difficulty lay in restraining himself from declaring himself to her there and then, and clasping her, as he longed to do, to his breast.

The thought of what she might suffer at the hands of Beauchamp filled him with dread and anger, and he was not blind to the peril in which she still stood. If anything were to go wrong with their plan, she might be taken, bound hand and foot like a felon, across the seas to France, there to face the mockery of a trial and the horror of death under the guillotine's knife. They must make sure, he told himself grimly, that nothing did go wrong. At all events, he determined that if it came to it he would shoot Beauchamp down like a dog, or strangle him with his bare hands, before he allowed him to harm one hair of Eugenie's head.

Eugenie, sublimely unaware of the torrential course of his lordship's thoughts, watched the play with interest, having always been very fond of the theatre. In the first interval she turned eagerly to the Earl to discuss it with him, giving him, had she known it, a severe test of mental dexterity as he endeavoured to conceal from her the fact that he had not seen any of the action and had not the least idea what the play was about.

St Osyth's decision not to tell Eugenie about the plot and counter-plot, though taken for the very best of reasons, gave rise to complications he had not forseen.

Beauchamp was feeling pleased with himself. St Osyth had snubbed him too often, had too often showed a public contempt for him, and he was determined to strike back at him in as devastating way as he could. That Freed arrogance, that superb self-assurance, would be shattered, and he would regret that he had ever curled his lip at Lambert Beauchamp and told him that he was not a gentleman.

Beauchamp had not missed the look of tenderness in the Earl's eyes as he looked at Eugenie at the charity ball, and it had given him a weapon more deadly than he had ever hoped to possess. He had known St Osyth a long time – if not intimately, at least by continuous observance and reputation – and he was aware that, while the Earl had had many pleasant little interludes with ladies on the town, he had never, by the age of two-and-thirty, shown any inclination to be in love with anyone. When a man of that stamp, who had reached the years of discretion, fell in love with a woman of breeding, it was a serious affair indeed, as Beauchamp well knew. The less susceptible a man was, the harder and more completely he succumbed once his defences were down, and the love of that sort of man in mature years was likely to be a once-in-a-lifetime thing which would affect his whole life and, inevitably, his judgement. The loss of such a love would bring pain, from which the victim might never recover. That was the sort of hold Beauchamp had always wanted over those he considered his enemies.

His plan was simple. He would capture Eugenie, and demand a large ransom from the Earl for her return. St Osyth, deeply in love as he was, would not fail to pay a very large sum of money indeed for the safe return of one who meant everything to him; and once he had the money safe, Beauchamp would deliver her up to Robespierre. Her death would then be certain, and not only would Beauchamp receive a second payment for her from the Tribunal, but he would also have the exquisite pleasure of knowing that St Osyth would spend the rest of his life suffering agonies of the most poignant grief.

His only problem had been how to come upon her in a situation where he could safely snatch her away. In London it was almost impossible, for she had so far shown no inclination for visiting places like the Vauxhall Gardens, where the presence of crowds was counterbalanced by the numerous shady alcoves into which couples retired for privacy. The news that she intended to make a journey to Kingston presented his first – and possibly his only – chance, and he had not wasted a moment in devising a plan and seeking out suitable accomplices.

It was fortunate that he had made friends, before there was any question of an ulterior motive, with Sebastian Freed, who combined a poor head for wine with a loose tongue. Beauchamp had a lifetime's experience in directing people to talk about the matters in which he was interested, while maintaining an appearance of complete indifference. He knew, thanks to McKendrick, the date and time of the journey, and the route she would take; from Sebastian, whom he knew from his observations to be in Eugenie's pocket, he would learn how she would be attended on the journey.

To Brooks's he therefore repaired, with a fair surety that Sebastian would turn up there at some point in the evening. His plan then was to encourage Sebastian, if he was not already three-parts foxed as usual, to drink himself into a suggestible condition, and then invite him back to his lodgings for a few quiet hands of piquet. Sebastian fancied himself a card-player and could never resist gambling, and piquet was one of the few games at which an expert playing with an amateur could be fairly sure either of winning or losing, as he required. Beauchamp meant to loose, slowly but steadily. Sebastian would thus be encouraged to play on, drinking more, winning small but useful sums of money, and experiencing ever stronger feelings of affection towards his companion and apparent victim. In that mood, as Beauchamp knew from a lifetime of manipulating people, he could be relied upon to tell Beauchamp anything he wanted to know.

The following day, Sebastian went to call on Eugenie. He had stayed so late at Beauchamp's lodgings, that it had not seemed worth his while to go to bed. Having bathed, shaved and changed his clothes, he went straight round to Brook Street, which meant he reached Berrington House in time to catch Eugenie before she went out.

'Where are you bound, ma'am? Can I go anywhere for you, or with you?' he asked her civilly.

'Only as far as Bond Street,' she replied with a smile. 'To Asprey's, on an errand for Lady Mary, delivering some instructions over the resetting of some stones. But you may give me your company along the way, if you please. Lady Mary does not like me to walk unattended, and a footman is no company at all. They dislike walking so much, poor things, that it makes me feel quite guilty.'

149

'With the greatest pleasure,' he said, and they set off, with Marie walking a pace or two behind.

'You are abroad very early,' Eugenie said, to make conversation. 'I have heard your cousin say so often that you are never out of bed before midday.'

'Well, I'm hardly ever *in* bed before seven, and a man must sleep some time,' he said with an engaging grin. Eugenie shook her head.

'What can you find to do until such an hour?'

'Why, play cards, ma'am. The delights of gaming increase after midnight, for some reason! Last night, for instance, I dropped in at Brooks's some time after eleven, met up with an acquaintance, went back to his rooms, and played piquet until six o'clock. That fellow Beecham, actually, the one Max disapproves of so violently. Well, I suppose he has his reasons; but he'd be glad to know that I got a little of the family's own back last night. Played cards with him for five hours, and lost only one hand. Came out fifty guineas to the good, ma'am, so I count it time well spent. Why, what's the matter? Are you unwell? You look quite upset.'

'Beauchamp – that man!' she whispered, her hand at her throat. 'You were with him all night?'

'Oh, there's nothing in that, I assure you,' he said, puzzled. 'He ain't quite out of the top drawer, I know, and Max don't think him quite the thing, but he's not a bad fellow, take him for all in all, and one can't cut a member of one's own club, after all! There's no harm in him, if you know how to handle him. He paid up like a man last night, though by what I hear he's in pretty queer stirrups – been far up the river Tick for months past, and going down for the third time, so some say.'

'But – but is it possible you don't know?' Eugenie said in an urgent undertone. 'Can you really not know who he is?'

Explanations followed, and Sebastian's amiable face clouded over. 'Well, now,' he said furrowing his brow, 'that puts a different complexion on things altogether. And, come to think of it, you did come up in conversation rather a lot last night.'

'He asked questions about me?'

'Well, I can't recollect that he asked questions, but he seemed interested whenever I spoke about you. Thought it was just politeness at the time, but if he's what you say he is, that accounts for it.'

'But what were you saying about me?' she asked urgently. 'You must try to remember. What did you tell him?'

'Lord, ma'am, nothing in particular that I can remember! Nothing he wouldn't be likely to know anyway. I can't really recall any details – we were playin' cards, you know, and one's mind was on other things.'

'You may be sure his was,' Eugenie said bitterly. 'If you wish to help me, you must remember what you told him about me.'

'Wait, let me think,' Sebastian said, frowning with the effort. 'Wait, yes, I remember now – I was talking about how well you'd settled down, and how many friends you've made – '

'The McKendricks!'

'Yes, I did mention them, I think. I remember now he said it was admirably generous-minded of you to maintain a friendship with people not of your order. Agreed with him – not but what you wouldn't always do what was right, of course.'

'You told him about my proposed visit to the McKendricks' house,' Eugenie groaned.

'Lord, no, ma'am, why should I do that? I ain't a spouter. The conversation was quite general, I assure you,' Sebastian said hastily. 'Besides, now I come to think of it, he knew about it already. *He* told *me*, in fact. I didn't say a word.'

But Eugenie could not accept the assurance. It was clear to her that a great deal of drinking had gone on as well as talking, and she had no doubt that in the course of it Beauchamp had learned all the details of her travel arrangements that he could need.

'What am I to do?' she said miserably.

'Cancel the visit, for certain,' Sebastian said. 'It will be too dangerous to risk it.'

'But that would be such a dreadful slight to the McKendricks! They would think I had grown too proud for them. And besides, if he does not strike at me then, he will find some other occasion. He will not give up so easily. Must I live the rest of my life in fear?'

Sebastian's heart swelled with remorse and chivalry. 'No, indeed, ma'am, not while I have breath in my body. It's clear this man must be put out of the way of harming you once and for all – and if I have been the one to put you in danger, then I must be the one to recoup the situation.'

'But how?' Eugenie asked. 'Nothing you say to him will stop him. There is nothing you can threaten him with.'

'I don't mean to threaten him. I have just this moment thought of a capital plan for putting a spoke in his wheel. It's a sure-fire winner. Listen!' And halting on the corner of Conduit Street, his eyes gleaming with laughter and excitement, he told her of his idea.

Chapter Ten

The roads leading out of London had for some years been
growing notoriously bad, not so much from the point of
view of their poor going, for that was much the same
everywhere, but from the likelihood a traveller faced of
being robbed. There were, indeed, some stretches of road
across which it was unsafe to travel without an armed
guard; where bands of mounted robbers waited almost
openly for victims. It was for that reason, in the first
place, that McKendrick had advised Eugenie not to take
any of the more obvious routes to Kingston, for they all
passed through areas well known for this hazard. The
road which passed through Brentford and wound along
the Middlesex bank of the Thames might be longer and
less frequented, but there were little scatterings of houses
all along it, and it passed through none of those empty
heath areas beloved of highwaymen. The woods at Marble
Hill, where Beauchamp had chosen to set up his ambush,
were in fact the only place he could have mounted such
an attack.

On the day of Eugenie's journey to Kingston, Buckland,
the Earl's groom, rode out early to the woods to reconnoitre, and returned to his master with very satisfactory news.
There was a place, where the woods were densest, where
a tree trunk was lying half-across the road.

'Whether naturally or not I couldn't say, my lord,'

Buckland said impassively, 'but it narrows the way so that while it wouldn't trouble a horseman, a coach would have to slow right down to manoeuvre round it.'

'That sounds like the place,' St Osyth nodded. One anxiety, that they might wait at the wrong place, was allayed.

'Not a doubt of it, my lord.'

'Any sign of anyone?'

'No, my lord. All quiet.'

'You could find this place from another direction, through the woods? We dare not approach along the road, in case they are already in position by the time we get there.'

'Yes my lord. I took the precaution of surveying the ground a little.'

'Very well,' said St Osyth. 'I think we should make our preparations to start. We don't know when they'll take up their positions, and it would be better if we could be there before them.'

St Osyth was reasonably sure that Beauchamp's force would consist only of himself and the three men Martin had seen him interviewing. As he did not know his plan had been discovered, he would not expect more than a coachman and a couple of footmen to be guarding the two women on the journey, and would reason that with guns and surprise on their side, four would be enough. Also, the more men Beauchamp employed, the more it would cost him, and men such as those would inevitably demand to be paid at least half their fee in advance.

The Earl decided, therefore, to keep his own force down to the four of them – himself, McKendrick, Martin and Buckland – since with the help of the coachman and footmen, they would then outnumber the villains. The larger his own force, the harder it would be to hide, and above all he did not want to scare Beauchamp off. He must be taken in the act, or he could not be rendered harmless.

The dinner to which Eugenie had been invited would

not, in fact, take place. McKendrick had cancelled, or rather, postponed it the night before, using to his wife the excuse of a slight indisposition on the part of Eugenie, and to his guests an indisposition on the part of his wife. He had sent the letters of apology and excuse by hand only the evening before so that there was no likelihood of the conspirators hearing of the cancellation.

The dinner was meant to begin at three o'clock, and the carriage would therefore leave Brook Street soon after noon. The conspirators, unless they were watching the house, which St Osyth thought unlikely, would not know that, however, and so it was certain that they would take up their positions well in advance of the earliest time they thought the carriage might pass. St Osyth's party therefore set off just before ten o'clock, with the certainty of a very long and weary wait ahead of them; but three of the four, at least, were buoyed with a fierce determination and a righteous anger which, if there were justice in the world, would greatly mitigate their suffering.

Sebastian's plan was simplicity itself, in which lay its sole advantage over common sense. It was not his original plan, but he had not been able to persuade Eugenie to adopt his original plan, which had been that he dressed up as her and took her place in the carriage beside Marie, while she remained safely at home until he returned with the despicable Beauchamp trussed up like a chicken and turned him over to justice.

Eugenie refused absolutely to allow her maid to face a danger which she was to be protected from.

'But Marie wouldn't be in danger,' Sebastian pointed out. 'Beauchamp doesn't want *her*, you know!'

But Eugenie could not be persuaded. She had never forgotten how her great-aunt's maid, Solange, had been executed alongside her mistress when she had been guilt-less of any crime except obeying her mistress, as she was bound to do. 'Besides,' she said, 'if there are to be firearms, there is no knowing where the balls may go. I cannot send Marie to face such hazards while I avoid them.'

Sebastian was therefore forced to come up with another plan, and upon the whole, he thought it would do just as well, though it represented more danger to Eugenie. In this scheme, he would dress as a woman and change places with Marie, concealing his pistols under his cloak. The kidnappers would order the women to get out of the coach, and he would make sure that he descended first, and then step aside as if to make way for Eugenie. The kidnappers would naturally have their eyes on her, and would not notice him taking out his pistols until it was too late.

'They will be surprised, you see,' he explained kindly to Eugenie, 'and that will be everything! Once I have them off their guard, the coachman and grooms will help me and we'll do it between us.'

His own man, Handley, would come along behind with a horse and trap, bringing Marie with him. He was to keep far enough behind not to put the conspirators on their guard, but close enough to render assistance if Sebastian had not already overcome them by the time he arrived. Marie would then take her place in the carriage and the two women could go on to Kingston, while Handley and Sebastian took the felons back to London in the trap, to be cast into prison.

Sebastian could not help feeling, rather proudly, that he had thought of everything. Eugenie, however, could not help feeling that the whole thing was very hazardous, but that it was better than doing nothing. She insisted that the coachman and footmen should be warned of what was to happen, in case the surprise should render them so frozen with astonishment that they could not help at the right moment. She also suggested that Handley should bring not only Marie but a couple of stout men with him.

Sebastian was wounded. 'Do you think I can't handle that villain on my own?' he enquired rhetorically.

'But consider,' Eugenie said urgently, 'you do not know how many men Beauchamp might have with him. He will not attempt to hold up a carriage all on his own. Suppose there are six of them, or ten?'

Sebastian scoffed at her fears, but agreed at last to the modification. As far as his disguise was concerned, it was left to Marie to find a dress for him. He was a small and slight man, and would do very well as a woman, but both Marie and Eugenie were diminutive, and their dresses would have been too small. She borrowed one from a friend in Brompton, and when it had been let down a little at the hem and out a great deal at the waist, it fitted well enough. Sebastian was to wear it over his own clothes, so that he could cast it off when it had served his purpose. A cap over his hair and a cloak with a hood completed the disguise, which would not have borne close scrutiny, but was not, of course, intended to.

On the day of the dinner, Eugenie and Marie bid farewell to Lady Mary and went down to the carriage under the watchful eyes of Treese and the porter. The carriage moved off, and when it reached Piccadilly it pulled up outside Beresford's, the haberdashers. Marie descended from the coach and went inside, as if to perform some last-minute errand. A few moments later, 'Marie' returned and climbed into the coach, and it went on its way again. If anyone had been watching five minutes later, they would have seen a diminutive woman in a drab pelisse come out of the shop and climb into a waiting cart, which then started off in the same direction as the carriage.

Seldom before in their history could Marble Woods have been the object of so much interest and activity. The road from the village of St Margaret's Ferry passed through its upper end on the way to Strawberry Vale, and there the woods were at their thickest. The lower part of the wood, where the ground became wet and marshy, thinned out into an area of scrub willow and rush bordering the river

Thames. On the other side, lush watermeadows rolled, peaceful with grazing dairy cattle, to the village of Petersham, on the edge of the great expanse of Richmond Park.

On their arrival, St Osyth's party waited at a distance with the horses while Buckland went forward on foot to reconnoitre, and it was as well that they did so, for Buckland returned to report that early as it was, the conspirators had already taken up their positions by the fallen tree. St Osyth had expected them to be waiting on the northern side of the road, where the trees were most dense, but in fact they had taken up position on the lower side. The presence, glimpsed by Buckland through the trees, of a waiting chariot and pair explained this. Obviously Beauchamp meant to bundle Eugenie into the carriage and drive off with her towards Richmond, and a quick departure would be prevented by the density of the woods on the northern side.

'Well, it's all to our advantage,' St Osyth said. 'It gives us much better cover, and places us uphill of them.'

With great caution the four men made their way forward until they were in sight of the road, and took up positions well hidden amongst the trees, but with a good view of the fallen trunk. They could see nothing of their quarry, and had not Buckland assured them they were there, they might have thought they had arrived before them. A long and nerve-racking wait ensued. The road was little used, and time dragged by, without even the variation of a false alarm to ease the tension which stretched their nerves almost to breaking point. There was nothing to do but keep still and watch, and again and again the waiting men had to deal with cramped limbs and pins and needles in the feet, moving cautiously to ease them without making a sound which might alert the villains to their presence.

At about one o'clock there came the sound of wheels, and everyone half-rose, alert, straining their ears. But Buckland caught his master's eye and shook his head, and his judgement proved sound. It was a farm cart, drawn by a single horse and led by a labourer. He cursed the fallen tree, but led his horse round it easily enough, the cart's inner wheels bumping over the thinner branches. He had been travelling only at human walking pace, but it was obvious that a carriage drawn at a smart trot by four well-bred horses would have to pull up in order to manoeuvre round the obstacle. St Osyth nodded grimly to himself, perfectly sure that the tree had not arrived in that position by accident.

Half an hour later, at about the time they were expecting the carriage to arrive at the spot, there was another false alarm, this time in the form of two men, probably a farmer and his son, who came trotting along on horseback. The man said something to the youth about the tree and waved his crop in a comprehensive gesture while riding his horse round the end of it, and the boy replied with a laugh, and spurring his horse to a canter, lightheartedly jumped it across the centre of the trunk. St Osyth watched with envy, wishing his own heart and mind could be so free from oppression at that moment. He settled down again to wait. Glancing to his right, he could see Buckland checking the priming of his pistol once more. To his left he saw McKendrick, who looked tense and nervous, wiping his upper lip and then his palms with his handkerchief. Martin should have been beyond him, but St Osyth couldn't see him, and frowning he raised himself a little to see better.

It was at that moment that the carriage came into sight, and every other thought was instantly driven out of the minds of the watchers. As soon as the coachman saw the tree, he pulled the horses from a trot to a walk, and on reaching the obstruction, halted the horses so that the groom beside him could get down to lead the horses round it. Then everything happened at once. Two masked men burst from the trees in front of the carriage, brandishing guns, and a shout from one of them demanded that the coachman and groom put their hands in the air and keep still. It was obvious that neither of them was Beauchamp, and nor was a third man who came out of the trees behind the vehicle and shouted a warning to the footman who was about to climb down from his seat behind.

Buckland and St Osyth were keeping very still, waiting only for Beauchamp to appear before making their move, for so far nothing had been accomplished from their point of view. But poor McKendrick was in a dreadful state of nerves, not only from the long wait and his dreadful feelings of responsibility for Eugenie's safety – for he could not help feeling that it was his fault that she had been placed in this danger, whatever St Osyth said – but also from his strong legal instincts which were now being outraged by the sight of armed men holding up a coach at pistol point. He half rose from his position, and the movement caught the eye of the third masked man, who swivelled his pistol from the footman towards this new hazard. McKendrick's finger on the trigger of his pistol had been crooked for a long time and had grown somewhat numb: he exerted, without meaning to, just too much pressure with it, and the pistol went off with a shattering report.

Probably in simple reaction, the third man whipped round and fired at McKendrick, who cried out and reeled backwards, and fell down amongst the bushes, out of sight. It was at that very moment that Beauchamp had at last emerged from the trees right opposite the door of the carriage and shouted something angrily at his own man, who had broken the rule he had laid down about firing. As if in response to his voice, Buckland and St Osyth, moving as one man, stepped forward out of the trees, their pistols prominent, and shouted to the villains to drop their weapons.

At the same moment the carriage door opened, and a cloaked woman jumped out and with a hoarse shout flung herself in Beauchamp's direction, only to be felled by a blow from the butt of the pistol of the third masked man, who was still standing by the rear wheel, covering the footman. The footman, seeing his chance, flung himself down from his seat on top of the masked man, and they wrestled briefly on the ground, until the villain managed to hit his attacker with the butt of his pistol, first on the shoulder, rendering him helpless, and then with a second blow to the skull, knocking him unconscious.

As soon as the footman had moved, the coachman and groom had drawn out their pistols and pointed them triumphantly at the two masked men, who seeing themselves outnumbered two to one, lifted their hands in surrender. Buckland and St Osyth were running forward from the trees, and the danger seemed to be over. But the door of the carriage was open, Beauchamp was barely a foot away, and no one's pistol was pointing at him. He darted forward and grabbed Eugenie's wrist, hauling her body from the carriage, and as she fell forward, he ducked under her, catching her about the knees and throwing her over his shoulder like a bundle of washing. She screamed and struggled, and the coachman and groom instinctively turned their pistols towards the new activity.

'Don't shoot, for God's sake! You'll hit her!' St Osyth cried out in desperation. The groom's gun went off at the same instant, the shot thudding into the ground a foot behind Beauchamp, who was already running, awkwardly but with amazing speed considering his burden, back into the trees. The two villains, taking advantage of the moment, made a run for it, while the third masked man drew his second pistol from his belt and fired it at the groom before following Beauchamp. St Osyth, managing at that moment to get past the horses, who were panicking and throwing their heads around in fright at the sound of shooting, fired back at the third man, but as shots came from the direction in which the other two villains had gained the cover of the trees, he was forced to jump backwards into the shelter afforded by the open carriage door.

The horses were by now almost uncontrollable and the coachman was struggling to hold them alone, the groom being unable to help him, for the third man's last ball had hit him in the arm. Buckland's instincts proved too strong for him, and he went to the leaders' heads instead of running after the villains. Four shots having been fired from the trees, St Osyth guessed there would be no more, and he ran in the direction Beauchamp had taken, shouting to Buckland to follow him. Buckland, his hands full of half-rearing carriage horses, hesitated, looking about him agonisingly for help, but there was none. McKendrick was somewhere in the trees to the far side, the groom was moaning and ashen, clutching his wounded arm, the footman was lying unconscious in a crumpled heap across the body of the maid, and Martin was nowhere to be seen.

'Go on, sir, go on!' the coachman cried nobly. 'I'll manage. Go on, for God's sake! Save the young lady!'

And at that moment Handley and the cart appeared at a gallop, rocking wildly round the bend in the road. He had heard the shots from afar and having whipped up his horses, now had to haul hard on the reins to stop them before they ran into the back of the carriage. The speed with which he had come to the rescue was laudable, but as it turned out, was their undoing, for as he arrived at the scene, the chariot and pair into which Beauchamp had flung Eugenie burst out of the trees behind them and raced off in the direction from which they had just come. Had Handley been just a little slower, they would have found themselves face to face with him, and he might have stopped them. As it was, St Osyth ran out from the trees and fired a last, useless shot at the vehicle as it disappeared, and then, in a rare moment of helpless despair, flung his hands over his head and groaned aloud.

The situation was as bad as it could be, for their horses had been tethered at some distance so that they wouldn't alert the conspirators to their presence. With the arrival of help, Buckland abandoned the carriage horses' heads, and raced away as fast as he could through the trees to fetch them, for their only hope now was to ride in pursuit of the chariot and try to overtake it. The cart was no use in that respect. Even though turning it round would have been quicker than running for the riding horses, it could never have overtaken the faster vehicle.

St Osyth, seeing Buckland run, understood what he was about, and took a few moments to assess the situation. Handley had brought two grooms with him, who were staring about them with eyes like saucers at all the lifeless bodies, and the Earl curtly ordered them to close their mouths and make themselves useful by holding the horses. The presence of Marie in the cart gave the Earl a moment of deep perplexity, which was resolved when examination revealed the true identity of the woman who had jumped down from the carriage. The footman had recovered his senses and was trying to sit up, a difficult process on account of both his swimming head and his bruised and aching shoulder. Sebastian, the cap tumbled from his head, was still unconscious. St Osyth knelt to examine him, and though his careful fingers found no evidence of a serious fracture, they came away with blood on them. The cap and the thickness of Sebastian's hair had protected him a little, together with the fact that he was moving as he was struck so that the blow had only glanced him. Had it struck him square, St Osyth thought grimly, his skull might well have been stoved in.

With a groom holding his horses, the coachman was able to give his attention to his wounded friend, who had taken a ball in the upper arm. It proved to have passed through the fleshy part without breaking the bone, which was extremely lucky. Seeing he was being attended to, St Osyth recollected McKendrick, and had just started towards the place where he had last been seen when McKendrick himself appeared, walking rather unsteadily down towards them, his hand at his head and blood trickling down his face. St Osyth examined him hastily, and found that the ball – a lucky shot at that distance – had creased McKendrick's scalp. Almost at the limit of its flight, it had no more than made a flesh wound which, though bleeding profusely, was in no way dangerous. It was probably pure fright which had caused poor McKendrick to faint dead away.

'What happened?' he asked feebly. 'Has he got her? Oh God, it's all my fault! We must go after her!'

'Where's Martin?' the Earl said grimly. 'I haven't seen him since before it all began.'

McKendrick didn't seem to hear him. He grasped the Earl by the shoulder and almost shook him in his anxiety. 'We must go after her! Why are you standing here? Why don't you do something? Oh God, oh God, I should never have allowed this insane plan to go ahead! I should have stopped you! Now he's got her and – '

'Be quiet,' the Earl said fiercely. 'Pull yourself together. Buckland is fetching the horses, and he and I will go after them. You must stay here and take care of the situation. My cousin lies there hurt, I don't know how badly, and two of the men are wounded. I have to leave you in charge.'

McKendrick swallowed, and took control of himself. His face was even whiter than its usual marble hue, but he said in almost a normal voice, 'Yes, my lord, I understand. I will take everyone back to your house in Grosvenor Square and wait there until you send word. If you need help, send to me, and I will arrange it.'

'Good man,' St Osyth said briefly as Buckland came through the trees, mounted, and leading the other horses. The Earl ran towards him and vaulted into the saddle, Buckland threw the reins of the other horses to McKendrick, and then the two men spurred forward and galloped away down the road in the direction the chariot had taken. McKendrick watched them go and murmured from the heart, 'God send they find her!' and then turned his attention to the unpleasant task of sorting out the muddle.

It was Sebastian's misfortune that, like his cousin, he had expected the attack to come from the right side of the road, where the woods were thickest, and for that reason he had positioned himself on Eugenie's right. When the men had come out of the trees from the left, he had seen the first two, but not the third man, who came up behind and out of his line of vision. Then Beauchamp had appeared, and Eugenie had instinctively shrunk back at the sight of him: all Sebastian's chivalric instincts had been aroused. He had flung himself into the breach, and had never seen the man whose blow felled him. By leaving the door open between Beauchamp and Eugenie, he had precipitated the disaster he had intended to prevent. The only point in which fortune was with him was that the blow had not killed him, and had given him such a concussion that he remembered nothing of what had happened even after he had regained consciousness.

McKendrick had performed the thankless task of sorting out the muddle at Marble Woods, and getting everyone back to Grosvenor Square. He had summoned a surgeon to attend to the wounded, and sent off a messenger to his wife with a letter which explained as much as he could tell her without risking her health in her condition. He thought it wiser not to send word to Lady Mary yet, but dispatched Handley, as being the most reliable of those left him, with letters to deliver to the constables of St Margaret's Ferry and Petersham and the magistrate at Richmond, explaining what had happened and requiring them to look out for any sign of the chariot or the villains.

After that there was nothing he could do but wait, in a state of the most wretched guilt and apprehension, for news. He wished he could be active himself, and cursed Martin for being absent at the time when he could have been most useful in taking over his vigil and freeing McKendrick to do something more positive. The mystery as to what had happened to Martin was absolute. They had searched the woods for him before leaving, thinking that perhaps he might have been struck by a stray shot, but there was no sign of him.

It was very late before St Osyth and Buckland returned, after a long and fruitless search which had traced the chariot as far as the gates of Richmond Park and no further. They had been too far behind to overtake it, and the ground was too dry to have taken any useful impression of the wheels. Exhaustive enquiries had established at last from people it had passed, the route the carriage had taken. Once it had gone into the park, it seemed not to have been observed by anyone, and enquiries at the other gates could not establish for certain that it had left by any of them. St Osyth had given strict instructions to all the gatekeepers as to what to do if they should see the chariot, but he felt sure that having gone in by the Richmond Gate, the carriage had simply driven straight across and out on the other side, probably by the Roehampton Gate. From there it could easily make its way back into London, and mingling with other traffic on the road through Putney, Wandsworth and Clapham, it would not be particularly noticeable.

McKendrick had questioned the weeping Marie about Sebastian's presence in the carriage, and was able to tell St Osyth the whole story when he returned. The Earl listened in silence, his mouth grim, his eyes shadowed, his face white with tiredness.

'Mr Freed was seen by the surgeon, my lord,' McKendrick concluded, 'who diagnosed a concussion, and gave him a sleeping draught. He is asleep now, my lord, upstairs. Your butler had a bed made up for him. He doesn't remember anything about the events at the woods, and the surgeon says he may still not remember when he wakes in the morning.'

'It doesn't matter,' St Osyth said wearily. 'I am beyond taking him to task – the outcome has been too terrible for anger. He acted for the best, and the responsibility is mine, for not telling him what we had planned.'

166

'My lord, I blame myself,' McKendrick burst in, 'for not cancelling the engagement as soon as the danger was known.'

'No, no,' St Osyth said, laying a hand on his shoulder. 'You need not reproach yourself – you did all you could to persuade me to caution. The blame is entirely mine. It was I who insisted that we go ahead with this plan. With hindsight, it seems to me that I have been wickedly irresponsible. I shall never forgive myself, even if – ' He swallowed, unable to complete the sentence, and sank into a silence which was at least half exhaustion. McKendrick hated having to rouse him to effort.

'My lord, there is one more thing: I have not sent any message yet to Lady Mary. I thought it best to wait and see the outcome of your enquiries, but as it grows late, it must now be considered what her ladyship should be told.'

St Osyth sighed and drew himself together with a colossal effort, like a half-drowned man hauling himself out of the water. 'You were quite right, McKendrick. I had better go and see her myself. This is not something to be imparted by a servant or a proxy. I must tell her myself what I have done. And you – had not you better return home? Your wife must be in great anxiety.'

'I have sent a letter to her, my lord. I have not told her what has happened – I did not think it wise – but she will not expect to see me before tomorrow. I would prefer to stay, my lord, and be on hand, if you have no objection.'

'As you please,' the Earl said shortly. 'I shall be glad of your help. Buckland, come upstairs and help me change. I must go and see my aunt at once.'

Chapter Eleven

Martin had found the waiting as difficult as had the other
three, but being considerably younger than any of them,
had not been able to resist translating his restlessness into
action. Just before the two horsemen had come by, he had
left his station and crawled away through the undergrowth
until he was past the bend in the road, when he had scut-
tled across and made his way cautiously back to where the
chariot was standing, to examine it.

The horses, half dozing, jerked their heads when he
came out of the shadows, and one of them whickered to
him. He froze back against the trees, but there was no
alarm and after a moment he crept right up to the carriage
and looked inside. It appeared to be a normal job-chaise,
which had probably at one time been a gentleman's chariot
and been bought at second hand by the job-stables. It was
very shabby, the black paintwork outside chipped and
scratched; the upholstery inside, once a crimson brocade,
now much soiled and worn thin in some places and torn
in others.

He had just opened the door nearest him to examine the
inside more closely when the sound of McKendrick's shot
reached his ears: he started and turned to run towards the
ambush site. There were more shots, which told him that
things were not going as planned, and he cursed the ill
luck by which he was out of position when things at

last started to happen. But the events of the ambush followed one another so quickly that he had gone but a few yards when he heard a crashing through the undergrowth and Beauchamp appeared with Eugenie bundled over his shoulder, closely followed by a masked man in a drab driving coat with a pistol in his hand.

It was the work of instinct for Martin to fling himself behind the chariot before the men spotted him. Had Beauchamp been alone, he would have attacked him, but the other man, with his pistol already drawn, was too immediate a threat. If he so much as showed himself, he was perfectly certain that the man would shoot him on the spot, and any chance of saving Eugenie would be lost. His eyes almost starting from his head with horror, Martin watched through the glass of the carriage as Beauchamp flung Eugenie down from his shoulder. As her feet touched the ground the other man seized her in an iron grip, while with a few rapid movements Beauchamp ripped a kerchief from around his neck and gagged her with it, and then pinioned her arms against her body with the leather belt from around his waist.

In seconds she was helpless. The unknown man whipped off his mask, revealing himself to be the one-eyed man Martin had seen in the Dog and Duck, and clapped an old-fashioned tricorne on his head. With the greatcoat, this gave him the appearance of a coachman – rather a low one, but then the carriage was too shabby to be a gentleman's. Martin understood at once that he was going to drive while Beauchamp, who looked just too much like a gentleman to sit on the box unnoticed, rode inside and restrained Eugenie. His body reacted before his mind had even consciously assimilated these thoughts. He threw himself through the open door of the chariot and rolled under the seat, drawing his legs in just as the other door was opened and Eugenie was flung inside. Beauchamp scrambled in after her, snapped the door closed, and reached across to close the further door as the carriage lurched into movement.

All these things happened at great speed, and both men were acting almost without thought according to a prearranged plan, or the fact that the other door was open might have roused their suspicions. As it was, Beauchamp shut it automatically, and had he even noticed the circumstance, there would have been no time to act upon it, for they were fleeing for their lives. Eugenie had landed on her knees on the carriage floor, and as the carriage lurched and swayed over the rough ground, Beauchamp pushed her down onto her side and held her down with one foot. The carriage gave one more preposterous lurch as it gained the road, jerked round to the right, and began rattling and bouncing as the horses gathered speed. There was the sound of one more shot, and a muffled thud as it struck the back of the chariot, and they were away, free and clear.

Eugenie, flung down and unable, because her arms were bound, to save herself, had shut her eyes in instinctive reaction to the pain of hitting the floor. She was already bruised from the rough handling, and the gag was half suffocating her, while the leather strap cut cruelly into the soft flesh of her arms. She opened her eyes, and found herself looking at a pair of knees and lower legs, in worn kersey breeches and stockings with a neat darn running down one of them. These terminated in a pair of scuffed shoes decorated with pinchbeck buckles of unconvincing brassiness, the like of which it had never been her privilege to study at such close quarters.

Shock, partial suffocation, and the jolting she had received, prevented her from fully absorbing the implication of the legs for some moments. She supposed vaguely that they were the property of another of the kidnappers, and it did not immediately occur to her to wonder why he should choose to travel under the seat rather than on it. Then recovering a little, she craned her neck to look along the body, and came to a waistcoat, tastefully decorated with a brown smudge whose acquaintance she had already made. A gasp of mingled alarm and relief sounded muffled through her gag as, craning a little more, she found herself staring upside down into the wide and anxious eyes of Mr Thomas Martin.

The full realisation of her own danger came to her as she understood his. The single grunt which had escaped her had cost her a kick to the side of the head from Beauchamp, which, though it had been intended to warn rather than hurt her, told her that he intended to allow her no opportunity to escape or to call for help. If he discovered Martin, he would kill him, she felt sure, but she doubted whether Martin himself understood how ruthless a man he was dealing with, or he would never have done anything so foolhardy as to stow away under the seat of the carriage. There was barely room for him under there. At any moment he might be discovered; when the carriage stopped and she was taken out, he certainly would be. She tried to convey all this to him with her eyes, but he only gave her a wavering smile, which was intended to reassure, and rolled his eyes upwards towards her captor.

Martin knew his danger, but also knew that if he was to overpower Beauchamp, it must be while he was in the carriage with him, for here the odds were one to one. Once the carriage stopped, the one-eyed man would make it impossible for him to prevail. Martin had a pistol, of course, but he had to assume that Beauchamp also had one; besides, to shoot in such a confined space would be to risk hitting Eugenie. Beauchamp would know that, too. Martin's best, his only chance, was to wrestle Beauchamp into submission, but he was starting from a difficult position, confined under the carriage seat and behind Beauchamp's legs. If only Eugenie could help a little, even distract his attention. Martin tried to convey the message to her by rolling his eyes, even by mouthing at her, but she only stared at him, her eyes enormous above the stifling scarf, so that he wondered if she were really fully conscious.

Unknown to Martin or to Eugenie, Beauchamp had by now had the leisure to consider the implications of the open carriage door. It was possible that it had come open by accident, but unlikely, for carriage doors were designed to avoid that very thing happening. He glanced down at Eugenie, and saw that she was staring very hard at something under the seat, and a grim smile came over his face. Slowly, slowly he drew out his pistol and cocked it. A moment later Martin, who was beginning to lose the feeling in his arms, found himself staring into its twin muzzles at very short range.

'All right, out you come,' Beauchamp said grimly. 'Very slowly indeed, otherwise I shall have to try the effect of blowing your head off at close quarters. I imagine it would make rather an unpleasant mess.'

Martin extricated himself carefully. 'You wouldn't shoot in here,' he said, trying to sound confident about it. 'You might hit her ladyship.'

'And why should you think I'd mind that?' Beauchamp asked pleasantly.

'Because I know you don't want her harmed,' Martin said. Beauchamp scowled at him.

'Oh, you know that, do you? Then you know a deal too much. Squat down there, in that corner, where I can see you. Now then, what are you doing here? Wait, I know you – you're the little rat of a lawyer's clerk from Kingston! Playing knight errant, eh? Well, you'll very soon find out what a big mistake you've made, interfering with my business. I suppose you put those others on my tail.'

'Yes,' said Martin, seeing no reason not to sound bold. 'We know your entire plan. We have known all about it for weeks. We know everything about you and your cronies, and you can't possibly escape.'

'Can't I? And what's to stop me just putting a shot right through your head here and now?'

'It wouldn't do you any good if you did,' Martin said, hoping the tremble in his voice wasn't as obvious to Beauchamp as it was to him. It was a vain hope. A smile came over Beauchamp's face, which was not a nice thing to see.

'Well it certainly wouldn't do you any good, would it, mister lawyer's clerk? Or should I say, mister *former* lawyer's clerk!'

In that instant, Martin knew he was going to die. And in a desperate reaction he flung himself forward, grabbing Beauchamp's wrist with both his hands and forcing the pistol upwards. It went off with a shattering report, and as if in response, the carriage gave a lurch and shot forward. The two men struggled in silence for possession of the gun, Martin desperately forcing it always upwards, horribly aware of Eugenie's presence on the floor of the carriage, while Beauchamp fought to free his hand and to cock the pistol for its second shot. Eugenie cried out in pain, for Beauchamp was standing on her leg, and thrashed angrily, which for an instant threw him off balance. The pistol went off again, the sound deafening in the confined space.

Relief surged through Martin. Now Beauchamp had no more shots, and it was simply strength against strength. Martin let go with one hand to try to get his own pistol out from his pocket, where it was maddeningly tangled in the loose cloth. But the chariot's movements seemed to have grown more eccentric by the moment, and suddenly it lurched violently, as if a wheel had gone up a bank, tilted for a second at a fantastic angle so that it seemed as though it must crash right over, and then thumped back down level again. It had been enough to fling Martin sideways, and he had to release Beauchamp's arm in order to save himself from falling. In that instant, Beauchamp, his position more stable than his young adversary, took the opportunity to reverse the pistol and strike him a violent blow behind the ear. Martin groaned and slumped down on top of Eugenie.

That there was something amiss with the carriage was quite plain to Beauchamp. He wasted no time in examining Martin to see how badly he had damaged him, but staggered up to let down the right-hand window, thrusting his head and shoulders through to look ahead. They were in what appeared to be open country but which he guessed was actually the middle of Richmond Park. The horses had bolted and were galloping flat out, their ears laid back in panic. The one-eyed man was slumped over sideways on the box as though he were ill, the reins slack across his knee, his right hand hanging limply down beside him.

'Hi!' yelled Beauchamp. There was no reaction. 'Hi!' Still no reaction from the one-eyed man. 'Woah, boys, woah!' he called persuasively to the horses. They were slowing a little, but they were still cantering fast, and at any moment the carriage might go over. A glance behind him told him that Martin was beyond hindering him for the moment, and pushing the pistol back into his pocket, Beauchamp heaved himself through the window into a sitting position, grasped the top of the chariot, and pulled himself up until he was standing on the frame of the window, his upper body bent forward across the roof. Reaching across he grasped the rail on the far side of the roof, and kicking with his feet hauled himself out onto the top. From there it was not too difficult to crawl down onto the box and grab the reins.

The one-eyed man groaned, and it was then that Beauchamp saw the spreading stain on the back of his drab greatcoat. Now he understood! When the pistol had discharged itself, one or both of the balls must have passed through the louvres in the front of the chariot and shot his colleague in the back. Beauchamp snarled his frustration and rage. He had chosen the one-eyed man as being the most useful to him – because the most ruthless – for this stage of the plan, but wounded he was worse than useless, he was a hindrance. He seemed to be badly wounded, too: now barely conscious, and remaining in his seat partly through the inertia of his heavy body, and partly because his left hand was hooked round the rail of the weatherboard.

Beauchamp leaned forward and took hold of the hand. It was icy cold, and its grip was like that of a corpse. His teeth bared with determination, Beauchamp shook the reins and yelled to the team to send them on faster, and then finger by finger he unclamped the rigid hand of the one-eyed man, who groaned again and opened his good eye. Perhaps some premonition of danger penetrated the Lethe of his mind, for he began to struggle upright. But it was far too late. The last finger came free, and with a violent heave of his shoulder, Beauchamp toppled him from his seat. His cry was whipped away by the speed of the carriage, and cut short by the heavy thud as his body hit the ground. Lightened of his weight, the chariot jumped forward, and Beauchamp settled himself more securely on the driving seat and took a firmer hold on the reins. He had rid himself of his liability; now he must complete his plan on his own.

Eugenie had been knocked breathless when Martin landed on top of her, and with the impediment of the scarf in her mouth, she could not draw in enough air and for a moment she lost consciousness. When she came to herself again, the carriage was swaying and rattling in a way that suggested great, though not excessive speed. Martin was still lying across her, and her first concern was to try to extricate herself from under him. She was only partly successful. His inert body pinned her down, and without being able to use the leverage of her hands and arms, she was able only to roll him away from her so that her head and shoulders were free.

They were alone in the carriage, and the window was open to its fullest extent. Had Beauchamp jumped out? But why would he do that? She tried to think, though her mind felt numb and thick, as though her head were stuffed with wool. What had happened? Ah yes, the carriage had lurched violently. Something had gone wrong – the horses had bolted perhaps? Beauchamp had had to climb out to help control them. Oh, this was their chance, their one chance perhaps, she thought in desperation. If she could only rouse Martin, he could untie her bonds, and then they could wrench open the carriage door and jump out. For only the fraction of an instant did she consider the damage she would do to herself in jumping from a carriage travelling at full speed, before dismissing the fear. Her situation was desperate – she was in mortal danger. No proceeding was too extreme to consider if it gave her a chance of freedom.

But how to rouse Martin? He was deeply unconscious, his breathing thick and heavy. At any moment the emergency might be over, and the carriage might stop to allow Beauchamp to take his place inside again. Urgently she tried to call to him, making strange, strangled noises through her gag. She tried to shake him by wriggling her body, but she could barely move him, and her breathing was so restricted that violent effort threatened to make her lose consciousness again. She lay still to rest until the black flecks had gone from before her eyes, and then had an idea. Inch by inch, with great effort, she moved her upper body, wriggling herself round until her face was beside his. Then she moved her mouth until it was positioned over his ear and, through the cloth of her gag, she took hold of his earlobe between her teeth and bit it as hard as she could.

Martin groaned and muttered, but did not wake. She bit again, jerking her head back and forth to increase the effect, and then had to release him to gain her breath. She moved her head round until she could get hold of the end of his nose, and bit that. He moaned and tried to move away. She bit him again and he put up a weak hand to fend her off, and then gradually he came back to his senses.

Urgently through her gag she tried to talk to him, to

make him understand how important it was for him to act *now*, but his head was swimming, and it seemed an unbearably long time before he was properly aware of his surroundings. Then he started and tried to get up, only to sway and clutch his head as dizziness overcame him. Eugenie's noises were becoming desperate, and at last he understood their import and reached over with fumbling fingers to undo the scarf around her mouth.

'Thank God, thank God,' she whispered as the air flowed freely into her starved lungs. 'Quickly, untie me. We must get out.'

'What happened?' he asked in a grim mutter as he reached for the strap that held her arms.

'I don't know. You fell on me and I fainted just for an instant. But Beauchamp has had to climb out of the window. The horses must have bolted. At any moment he may pull up and get back in. We must jump out. Oh hurry, hurry!'

'Jump out! You must be mad!' he hissed. 'At this speed you would kill yourself.'

'It's our only chance!' she whispered urgently. 'Once he stops, he will kill you, and then I am lost. We must do it now. Oh!' as her arms came free at last. She tried to sit up, but had no feeling in her arms or hands, and could not use them to thrust herself up. Martin began rubbing them, to restore the circulation, and thought about what she had said. His mind was not working at full power, and he could not see an alternative. Once the carriage stopped, there would be two of them to face, and in all likelihood the one-eyed man would simply shoot him, it being the easiest way of rendering him harmless. But to jump from a moving carriage! If only he could think of another way . . .

'Better now,' Eugenie whispered urgently. 'Oh quickly, we must get out. It's our only chance!'

'All right,' he whispered in reply. 'We'd just better hope we land on something soft. Wait, while I look.' He crawled to the window and cautiously lifted his head to look out, afraid that one of the men glancing back might see him. The bumpiness of their progress was explained: they were not on a road, nor even a track. There was grass all around, and just ahead of them was the edge of a wood which they seemed to be going to skirt. The trees would offer them shelter, if they could get to them. He looked back and nodded to her, and she crawled quickly to his side. 'Ready?' he whispered. He turned the handle, lifted the latch, and felt the door tug against his hand. He held it closed until they came opposite the trees, and then flung it back and jumped.

He heard the crash as the passage through the air whipped the door back against the body of the chaise, and then the breath was smashed out of him as he hit the ground and rolled over, feeling grass and twigs and something sharp like a line of coldness down his face. There was a violent pain in his lower back, but it lasted only a second, an instant numbness following the hurt which enabled him to roll over again and onto his knees, the urgency of the situation demanding that he take control at once.

Eugenie was lying at a short distance from him, crumpled up on her face. She didn't move as he began crawling rapidly towards her. The trees were to hand, and the chariot ahead of them was already slowing, for the sound of their departure would have given them away. He thought he caught a glimpse of a white face looking back, and something in the back of his mind registered a gladness, but he had no time to think about it. He must get to her, and get her into the wood. Was she hurt? Was she dead? God, not dead, please! She had jumped, though – what courage! It only occurred to him then that he should have made her jump first, in case her courage failed her and she was carried on in the chariot without him. He reached her side and touched her. She stirred and tried to sit up, and then cried out with pain.

'My leg!' she cried. 'Oh, it hurts!' Her face turned

white with the pain. He saw it happen, an extraordinary phenomenon. He knew that his mind was working very oddly, slowing time down, noticing things he had no time to notice. 'I can't move it,' she said. He felt for it through her skirts. It was at a strange angle – broken perhaps? Oh, the chariot was slowing, slowing, they must get into the woods.

'I'll try to carry you. It will hurt. Are you ready?'

She bit her lip and nodded. He got his hands under her and tried to get up, but she was heavier than he had expected, and he lurched awkwardly. She cried out, and the sound lanced him, for he knew she would not have made a sound if the pain were not extreme. He got his feet under him, found his balance, and staggered forward towards the trees. They seemed very far away. He passed at last under branches, staggered further in, into the shadows. They would pursue him, of course. He changed direction, tried to zigzag. His breathing hurt him, burned like fire. He was growing dizzy again. His foot caught in something, he fell forward, and only by a miracle twisted sideways so that he didn't fall on her. She cried out again with the pain, and when he released her, she turned her head to one side and was sick.

'I'm sorry,' she whispered after a moment. 'I couldn't help it.'

'No, I'm sorry,' he said. 'Your leg's broken, isn't it?'

'I think so.'

'Let me try to straighten it. It oughtn't to be bent like that.'

She endured it without crying out, but when he had finished there was blood on her lip where she had bitten it. He sat down beside her, discovering that his body was trembling all over with shock, and that he was incapable of any further effort for a moment.

'You've cut your face.' Her voice came from far away in the darkness. He remembered feeling the coldness after he jumped: that must have been blood.

'They will come after us,' he whispered. 'We must try to hide. I wish I could carry you, but I can't. I'm sorry.'

'Can you find two strong sticks to tie to my leg, to hold it steady? Then I might be able to hop a little.'

He nodded, but found he couldn't walk, so he had to crawl on hands and knees. Why couldn't he find wood in a wood? It was a joke in poor taste. At last he found two longish pieces, though they were not very strong. He brought them back, every nerve straining for sounds of pursuit. 'It's the best I could find,' he said. Cloth? He took off his jacket and with trembling fingers ripped the left sleeve off his shirt. He couldn't manage the right one, and she had to help him. With the two shirt sleeves he bound the two sticks against her leg while she held it steady. The white skin was already purpling with the bruise. It's the first time I've ever seen a countess's leg, he thought absurdly.

'Put your jacket on, you're shivering,' she whispered.

'I think it's shock,' he said. The pain was beginning to rise like a scream in his lower back where he had felt the blow and the numbness. 'My back hurts. I think that's why I can't walk any more. To his astonishment he saw tears running down her face. 'What is it?'

She only shook her head. 'I'm sorry,' she said again. He sat down beside her and stroked her hands, and then froze as the first sounds of approach came to them through the woods.

'It's him!' he whispered. She gasped, and they clutched each other like terrified children.

Then two things came to him at the same moment, glad things like beams of sunshine through darkness. The first was the thing he had noticed subconsciously just after they had jumped – there was only one face looking back from the chariot, only one man on the box. Beauchamp was up there alone. At some point in the journey the one-eyed man had disappeared.

The other thing was that he had a gun, a loaded pistol

in his pocket. It was that which had caused the terrible pain in his back – he must have landed on it. 'It's all right,' he whispered to Eugenie. 'Look!' He pulled the gun out from his pocket. 'It's loaded,' he said. 'We'll just wait here. When he comes, when he gets near enough, I'll shoot him.'

'Do you know how?' she asked.

'Yes. It's all right,' he said. She didn't ask about the second man. He thought she was half fainting with fear.

Time slowed even more, and they sat through a strange dream of delirium, shivering with shock and pain, listening as the rustling sounds ebbed and flowed around them, as Beauchamp beat back and forth through the woods for them. The shivering receded, and a warm drowsiness began to creep over Martin. He knew he ought to struggle against it, but he felt so tired, so tired. He leaned against Eugenie's shoulder, and the pistol drooped in his fingers.

Darkness seemed to loom over him, and he started violently awake, to see Beauchamp standing in front of him, smiling like a devil.

'Found you, at last,' he said. 'That was a very foolish thing to do, you know. It might have killed you both.'

Martin's hands had turned to pastry, they wouldn't grip the pistol. He put it in his lap so as to use both hands to cock it. Beauchamp didn't seem at all perturbed, which upset Martin and made him want to cry. He wanted to shout out, why aren't you afraid? Why can't I make you afraid? Slowly he lifted the pistol. His hands shook so that Beauchamp seemed to dance in the sights like a string puppet, his smile as false and painted as a puppet's. Stop shaking! he screamed at himself. A vast effort held the gun still, its muzzle pointing at Beauchamp's heart. But he hasn't got a heart, a voice in Martin's mind told him. You can't kill a man with no heart. Still smiling, Beauchamp took a step forward.

'Better give me the pistol,' he said kindly.

'No!' cried Martin, and pulled the trigger. The explosion

sounded strangely flat in the open air, and the flash from the muzzle was quite orange against the darkness of the trees. Beauchamp seemed to spring backwards with both feet together, his hands flung wide, and then he keeled over, as silently as a felled tree, and lay still in the bracken.

The silence crept back, and after a while the birdsong began again.

'I killed him,' said Martin. He sounded vaguely surprised.

'Yes,' Eugenie whispered. 'I didn't think it was possible.'

Chapter Twelve

It was while the Earl was still changing that the butler came up to his room looking, as far as it was ever possible for a butler so to look, very excited.

'My lord, an individual has arrived and wishes to speak to you on a matter of great urgency.'

'What sort of an individual?' asked St Osyth, hesitating above a pair of silken smallclothes.

'A rustic, my lord. He will not state his business except to you.'

'I will come down at once. Buckland, throw those aside and hand me my buckskins again. This rustic individual may have news that requires acting upon.'

'God send he may, my lord,' said Buckland fervently, crouching down with the riding breeches.

The Earl hastened down to the book room, where McKendrick was pacing up and down, and a small and wiry man in earth-coloured clothes stood in a respectful but defiant attitude in the centre of the room, turning his cap round and round in his hands.

McKendrick turned with a glad face to the door as St Osyth entered. 'Ah, here is his lordship! Now perhaps you will tell us what you know. My lord, this man – '

St Osyth held up his hand. 'I'll hear it from his own lips, thank you, McKendrick. Well, my good fellow?'

'Are you the Earl of St Osyth?' the man demanded

suspiciously. Buckland drew in a sharp breath of dis-approval, but the Earl only grinned.

'Quite right, always be sure who you are addressing. Yes, I am he. How can I convince you? Would you take my butler's word for it? In thirty years no one has ever known him tell a lie.'

'No, no, that's all right,' the man said with rough shyness. 'I'll take your lordship's word for it. No offence meant, my lord, but this here is a matter of importance.'

'None taken, I assure you. Your name?'

'Dipton, my lord. I work in Richmond Park, assistant gamekeeper.'

'Richmond Park!' St Osyth cried triumphantly. The prospect of some new start raised his spirits enormously. 'Gentlemen, I have the feeling that we are about to learn something useful at last. What have you to tell me, Dipton?'

'Well, my lord, it's about this here body.'

'Body? A dead body, you mean?' McKendrick asked sharply.

'A corpuss, sir, that's right, my lord. I was a-walking back home from looking over my coops – the young pheasants, my lord, and the foxes do go for to take 'em this time o'year, however you lock 'em up. And two-legged foxes too – I don't know which is worse. Break into anything, they will.' McKendrick's mouth opened to protest, and closed again as St Osyth threw him a murderous glance. There was never anything to be gained from trying to hurry this sort of person. They would only confuse him.

'Indeed they will. And on your way home . . .' he prompted gently.

'That's right, my lord, like I was saying, that's when I found this man. A-layin on the ground, he was, face down, all crumpled up. He was in the bracken, my lord, and I thought at first he was a poacher what had fallen asleep waiting for dark, except it was a funny place to lay up, not enough cover, you see. And then I see how the bracken's all broken down, and I reckon he must 'a' jumped into it. And then I see the blood.'

'Blood? Where?'

'All over his coat, sir – my lord. He'd been shot in the back, my lord, and that's a fact.' Dipton pursed his lips. 'That's something I couldn't hold with, my lord, to shoot a cove in the back. Don't seem right, somehow. And then I reckons as maybe that's how the bracken got so broken. Someone shoots him in the back, and then brings him on a cart and throws him off, to get rid of him, like.'

'He was dead when you found him?'

'Stone dead, my lord. No mistake.'

'And where is he now?'

'He lies where I found him, my lord, and Parker's with him. Parker's the boy what helps the gatekeeper, my lord. See, when I found him, I didn't know what to do. Then I thinks, Joe Cole, he's a book-learned man, he'll know. So I leaves him there – the corpuss – just covers him over with some bracken, like, on account it didn't seem decent just to go off and leave him as he was. And then I goes off to find Joe Cole – '

'Who is Joe Cole?' McKendrick could not prevent himself from breaking in at that point. Dipton stared at him as if he were mad.

'Joe Cole? Well, it's like I was telling you, sir. I went to speak to him, on account he's a – '

'Book-learned man, I know,' McKendrick said through his teeth, 'but who is he?'

'The keeper o' Richmond Gate, o'course,' Dipton said with sturdy amazement that anyone could be unacquainted with this luminary of the Park. St Osyth gave McKendrick a sad shake of the head.

'How could you be so dull, McKendrick?' he said. 'Everyone knows that! So, may I tell your story for you, Dipton? Stop me if I go wrong. You went to find Joe Cole, and took him back with you to see the corpse, and he, knowing that I was looking for a kidnapper, said that you should come

187

and tell me about it as quickly as possible. Ah yes,' he forstalled Dipton and added, 'and Parker was despatched to stand guard. You may give me all the details as we go, but for the moment the important thing is to waste no more time. You did just as you ought, Dipton. I'm very grateful to you. You can take me straight to the place, I presume?'

'Yes, my lord.'

'You came on horseback?'

'Yes, my lord. Joe Cole lent me his grey mare. He said as how – '

'Excellent, excellent. Now, would you do me the kindness to go with Buckland here and help him to bring the horses round? You'll come with me, Buckland.'

'And I, my lord,' McKendrick said anxiously. St Osyth smiled.

'By all means, my dear fellow. I would not be so cruel as to exclude you.' Buckland and Dipton departed, and McKendrick resumed his pacing up and down.

'I wonder who it can be, my lord? Pray God it is Beauchamp. Shot in the back, he says. That sounds like a falling out amongst thieves.'

'It may be nothing to do with our case at all, of course,' St Osyth said, 'but somehow, I don't think so. Richmond Park! The carriage certainly went into it – but could it be, McKendrick, that it is still there? Why did I not think of it? How often has it been said that it's quite possible to get lost in the middle of the park? And though we looked for wheelmarks on the tracks, we didn't think that they might have left the track and gone into the rough. I'm a fool, McKendrick!'

'No, my lord,' McKendrick protested. 'Anyone would have assumed that the carriage drove across the park as the quickest way back to London. What other reason could he have for entering it?'

'I don't know,' St Osyth said grimly, 'but I mean to find out, if I have to search every yard of the park on my hands and knees. Come, are you ready? The horses should be round at any moment. So much time has been wasted already! God knows how long ago it was that Dipton found the corpse – not less than three or four hours, by my guess.'

'I wonder,' McKendrick said hesitantly as they passed through into the hall. St Osyth raised his eyebrows interrogatively. McKendrick's face was gloomy as he continued. 'It occurred to me to wonder yet again, my lord, what happened to Martin.'

St Osyth grimaced. 'You are unfailingly comforting, McKendrick.'

Exhausted as they were, they must have slept, for Martin was awoken by a cry from Eugenie to the realisation that it had grown quite dark under the trees. A low reddish light was filtering through the branches from the setting sun, but it had little power. He struggled to wakefulness. His head was throbbing bitterly, and his lower back felt numb until he tried to move, and then it woke to jangling pain.

'What is it, what's the matter?' he mumbled thickly. He reached for and found Eugenie's hand.

'I must have been sleeping,' she said in a faint voice. 'I thought Beauchamp was coming after us.'

Martin sat up and looked across to where he could see the soles of Beauchamp's boots sticking up from the undergrowth.

'No, he's dead, don't you remember,' he said. Eugenie gave a shuddering sigh.

'Yes, I remember. Thank God! But what are we to do now, Mr Martin? It grows dark. Do you know where we are?'

'No, ma'am,' Martin said, 'but we cannot stay here, that's for sure. We should never be found. We must try to find our way to some house or cottage and send a message to his lordship.'

'My leg is broken,' Eugenie reminded him. 'I cannot walk, I fear.'

'God, yes, I had forgotten. Does it pain you very much, ma'am?'

Eugenie shrugged the question away. 'You must leave me here and go alone, Mr Martin. There is no help for it.'

'I can't leave you here alone,' he said. 'I don't know how far I should have to go for help. I might be gone for hours!'

'What else is there to do?' Eugenie asked him. He looked into her face, and met the steady gaze of her dark eyes. She has such courage, he thought, more than any man he had ever known.

'Very well,' he said. 'But first let me see if I can make you more comfortable.' With difficulty he managed to move her a little way so that she could rest with her back to a broad tree trunk, and took off his coat, spreading it over her shoulders. 'I wish there was something else I could do for you,' he said anxiously.

'There is no help for it. I shall do well enough.' Still he gazed at her, biting his lip, and she prompted him gently. 'The sooner you go, the sooner you will be back.' He nodded and turned away, and heard her voice behind him say softly, 'God bless you, Thomas Martin.'

St Osyth straightened from his examination of the corpse with a frown of disappointment. It was certainly not Beauchamp; but to look on the good side, it was not Thomas Martin either. The Earl had not seen the faces of any of the conspirators, but Martin had described the man with the scarred face and the dead eye. This must be he, and from his general build and the coat he was wearing, it seemed likely he was the third masked man, who had followed Beauchamp back into the trees after he had snatched Eugenie, and covered his retreat.

If that were the case, then it would seem that the chariot had certainly come this way. But who killed him, and why?

St Osyth's guess was that it was Beauchamp who had shot him, simply as a way of getting rid of him and ensuring that he did not betray him at some later date. That would be like the treacherous villain. The bracken was very broken, as Dipton, with his gamekeeper's eye, had noted, which suggested Beauchamp might have thrown him from the carriage.

'Cast around, everyone,' he said. 'There should be wheelmarks or hoofprints nearby. The coach certainly passed this way.'

It was not the best of places for finding evidence of passage, being a mixture of bracken, scrub and lion grass, but at least it was better than trying to determine one mark from another on a well-frequented carriageway. Further on the ground was covered in dense, springy turf, and after a while Buckland called his master cautiously.

'Just here, my lord – I'm not sure, but it looks like wheel marks. If you look at it on the slant, my lord, you can just see – '

'Yes, indeed, you are right Buckland. Well done. This is the direction, then.'

It was slow work, and though it was near enough the longest day for it to stay light until well into the night, such close work needed better visibility than was now prevailing. Buckland and McKendrick did not fail in diligence, but the other helpers evidently thought it a hopeless task, and fell further and further behind, chatting together in low voices and longing to return to their homes and suppers.

At last they lost the trail, and even Buckland was beginning to think they had better call it off and return in daylight, when St Osyth, casting further afield towards the edge of the old plantation, gave a cry of triumph: 'Here! To me!' They hurried to his side, and looked through the gathering gloom. He pointed to an area where, being slightly lower than the surrounding land, the ground was soft enough to take an impression. There was a multitude of deer-slots, and crossing them a deep wheelmark and several hoofprints from a shod horse, so sharply dug that here and there a sod had been thrown up.

'They came this way,' St Osyth said.

'Going fast, my lord,' said Buckland. 'See how they cut the turf here, and here.'

Interest revived, and everyone began to search. Soon afterwards, rounding the corner of the plantation, they found the carriage itself. One door stood open on the empty interior. The horses, still harnessed to it, stood dozing, hind feet cocked, while the broken reins trailing beside them showed where they had trodden on them while attempting to graze. Buckland went to them and stroked them, examining their legs.

'I don't think they are lame, my lord. If he stopped here, it was not for that reason.'

'They have been here a long while, at all events,' St Osyth noted. 'We must be cautious from now on. Beauchamp may be anywhere about. We know he is dangerous, and we must assume he is armed.'

'But why would he stop here?' McKendrick asked. 'If he meant to hide her ladyship in the woods, why would he leave the carriage here, to give him away?'

'Be sure to ask him that, when we find him,' St Osyth said grimly. 'Now, quiet and caution – '

'My lord!' called Dipton at that moment from a distance. 'There's a man here.'

It was Martin, lying in the bracken at the edge of the woods, where he had collapsed again. St Osyth ran to him, and cradling his head, tilted to the young man's white lips the silver flask which Buckland handed to him. Martin revived, sipped, and choked a little, and then tried to start up in alarm, until he saw who it was that held him.

'No, no, be easy,' St Osyth said gently. 'You are safe now.'

'How did you get here, Martin? What happened?' McKendrick asked in astonishment. St Osyth gave him a look of exasperation, and revised the questions.

'Try to tell us, Martin: is her ladyship here? And Beauchamp? Is she still in his power?'

Martin looked up at him vaguely. 'Beauchamp's dead,' he said. 'I shot him.'

Relief surged through the Earl, and he asked, the more gently because the more anxiously, 'And the Countess?'

Martin shook his head. 'Back there. In the woods. I couldn't carry her. I was going for help.' He closed his eyes, exhausted. 'But you're here.'

'Carry her? Is she hurt?'

Martin shook his head again. 'Back there,' was all he could manage to say.

St Osyth beckoned to one of the helpers to come and take charge of the boy, and with a few terse commands he ordered the others to spread out in an echelon to search the woods. 'Whoever finds her, call out to me. Don't try to move her. She may be hurt.' And he plunged into the woods from which Martin had emerged.

It seemed a long time after Martin had gone before Eugenie heard anything, but she was aware that time in her situation would be hard to judge accurately. She was feeling chilly and sleepy, and her leg was throbbing, but otherwise she was not in too bad a case, except for her anxiety. There had been nothing else to do but to send Martin off for help, but she was aware that the blow he had received to his head had been more damaging than he realised, and she was afraid that he might wander in a daze or fall down and sleep, and not remember on waking where she was. If help had not come by morning, she decided, she would have to try to move herself, however difficult that might be.

She did not at first understand what the noise was. It sounded like a buzzing or a rasping noise coming from some distance away, but it did not grow any nearer, and she decided it was not a loud noise in the distance, but a lesser noise from nearby. At last she realised that it was coming from the direction of the place where Beauchamp's body lay, invisible now in the gloom. This was a very unwelcome thought. Could it be some animal, some night prowler, investigating? She strained her eyes and her ears in that direction. It was only very slowly that her unwilling mind came to the conclusion that the sound she could hear was a laboured and stertorous breathing.

But he was dead, he was dead! Martin had shot him in the heart. She had seen him fall. It was not possible, it could not be possible, that he was still alive. Her pulse was racing, and the thundering in her ears made it hard to hear. Now there was a different noise, a rustling, grassy sound, and in the half-darkness she thought she saw a movement. Cold fear grasped her heart as she saw that the impossible was happening: Beauchamp was sitting up, was trying to get to his feet.

She froze against her tree trunk. Pray God he would not see her! How could he still be alive? She must keep quite still, or he would see her. Would he hear her breathing? Surely he would hear the pounding of her heart! He was on his feet now, swaying like a drunken thing, his breath labouring and bubbling like an ancient bellows, and Eugenie's mind babbled frantic prayers for deliverance as he began to lurch towards her.

Step by step he swayed towards her. He had seen her, oh he had seen her! His dark pitted face seemed to grin with a mad delight as he bared his teeth in the effort to breathe. Surely he must be badly hurt, she thought. The effort of moving must be too much for him! She tried to move herself, but grinding pain followed instantly from her broken leg. Now he was before her, and he slumped down to his knees beside her, his harsh breathing close enough to ruffle her hair.

He made a sound in his throat that seemed like an effort at speech, and reached out his hands for her.

That was when she heard the other sounds, of a normal, healthy body beating its way through the wood. It could only be rescue, and she cried out, 'Here! Here I am! Over here! Oh help me, help me!'

Beauchamp made another horrible, animal sound and she beat at him frantically with her hands as he reached for her throat.

'Help me! Help me!'

'I'm coming!' came the voice, and seconds later St Osyth burst into the clearing.

'Stop!' gasped Beauchamp harshly, and to Eugenie's horror, the Earl obeyed him. Beauchamp was kneeling half beside, half behind her, and had a pistol held to her temple. 'If you take one more step, I will kill her,' he snarled, a desperate, wounded animal.

Something snapped in Eugenie: she began to laugh, and she saw St Osyth's face turn to her in incredulous horror. 'It isn't loaded!' she cried, unable to stop laughing. 'It isn't loaded, you fool!'

The Earl sprang across the clearing like a tiger, his hands like bands of steel as they seized Beauchamp and lifted him away from her, to fling him down into the bracken. And then he was on his knees beside Eugenie, feverishly kissing her hands, stroking the hair from her brow, cradling her head tenderly as she laughed and sobbed away the terror of the last few minutes.

'It's all right, I have you, you're safe now,' he cried. 'Oh my darling, my darling, it's all right. He shan't hurt you again.'

'We thought he was dead. Martin shot him. He should be dead,' she sobbed into his waistcoat. 'Perhaps no one can kill him.'

St Osyth released his lapels from her clutching fingers so that he could turn his head to look at Beauchamp, who was lying on his back where he had been thrown, and showed no signs of rising again. 'I think he is very near death, my dear one. Certainly he will never harm anyone again. But are you hurt? Why did you not run from him?'

Her hysterical fit was passing, and she answered him

in a voice which was shaky but almost normal. 'My leg is broken. Martin went for help. Did he find you?'

'We found him. Poor young man, he seems to be in a bad way.'

'It was he who saved me,' she said earnestly, looking up into St Osyth's face. 'I owe him a great debt.'

'I owe him a greater,' said the Earl.

'Well, ma'am, and how do you feel now?' asked St Osyth, presenting himself at the foot of Eugenie's bed. In an ocean of fresh linen bedclothes and a foam of lace wrappers, she looked very small, very dark and rather lost, but her smile was as full of life as ever, for which the Earl was extremely thankful. 'Marie tells me you have eaten a large breakfast, so I do not quite give up hope.'

'I feel as though I had been beaten all over with clubs,' Eugenie told him genially, 'and as though someone has exchanged my right leg for a stone column from a Greek temple – but apart from that, my lord, I am extremely well.'

'I am very glad to hear it,' St Osyth said, accepting the invitation of her gesture to sit beside the bed. He looked as though he had not slept for several days, she observed. She decided this gentler aspect suited him.

'Only I am very curious,' she said. 'No one will satisfy me. When I ask questions, everyone, even my dear Marie, tells me I must not worry about anything, and will give me no answers.'

St Osyth grinned. 'I feel for you, ma'am. There can be nothing worse than being protected against one's will. What would you know? I am prepared to answer all questions.'

'Then, at once, what of Beauchamp?'

'Dead. He was dying already when I came upon you both. The wonder of it is that he lived so long.'

'Ah, but how did he live at all?' Eugenie asked. The Earl had not failed to observe the access of colour to her cheeks at his unequivocal answer. In some illogical part of her mind she had conceived the notion that he could not be killed. 'I saw him shot, you know. Martin certainly shot him.'

'And most accurately, too,' St Osyth said approvingly. 'He is a fine shot – or danger made him so. The hole in Beauchamp's coat was right over the heart.'

'Then how – '

'What he did not know was that Beauchamp carried in his pocket something very dear to his heart: a gold snuffbox belonging to me, a family heirloom, which he had acquired by dishonest means, and which he valued as it gave him, so he thought, power over me. Look, I have it here.' He drew it out from his pocket, and held it out to Eugenie on his palm. With round, distressed eyes, she observed the shattered lid and the hole in the base where the shot had passed through. 'Gold is a soft metal, ma'am. It did not entirely prevent the ball from entering his body, but it impeded it so that it did not enter his heart. He died from its effects, but not immediately. After lying unconscious for some hours, he revived sufficiently to – '

'Yes,' said Eugenie hastily, forstalling him. She didn't like to think of those moments in the clearing. St Osyth drew back his hand and stowed the snuffbox in his pocket. 'Well, that was a curious thing, was it not?' she said mildly. 'And how is Mr Martin? Marie says he has a concussion.'

'The surgeon opines that only the astonishing thickness of his skull could have saved him from serious injury. A gross calumny, I fear, considering how bravely he acted.'

'He saved my life,' Eugenie said gravely.

'I'm glad you think so. He blames himself very much for your broken leg. He feels that if he had remembered his pistol sooner, you need never have jumped from the carriage.'

'*Tiens!* That is not his fault!' Eugenie said emphatically. 'Does one think clearly when one has been hit upon the head? If he had not hidden in the carriage, there would have been nothing to stop that man from taking me away.'

St Osyth looked grim, and suddenly ten years older. 'I had no such excuse, ma'am. I had every opportunity to think clearly, and all I could do was to place you in the most hideous danger . . .' Lady Mary had told him exactly what she thought of him, at very great length, three times now, but nothing his enraged aunt could say could make him understand more clearly than he already did the risks Eugenie had faced, and the danger from which she had emerged with no help from him.

Eugenie looked at him compassionately, understanding what he must be thinking. 'Do not, I beg, be blaming yourself, my lord. I knew what Beauchamp threatened, and you see, I did not withdraw myself! Your cousin and I made another plan, which I expect was what made a confusion. But at all events, if you had told me I was to be kidnapped and begged me not to go to Kingston, I should have refused to listen to you. One thing,' she added with a smile, 'you should know about me: I am very, very stubborn.'

'It is good of you to say so, ma'am,' St Osyth said, without in the least forgiving himself.

'You must believe me! Even my Papa could not make me mind him, you know. He did not want me to help him with his work against the revolutionaries, but I insisted. So you see it was all my own doing that this Beauchamp had any reason to try to kidnap me.'

'You wish to take all the blame yourself,' he said with an unwilling smile.

'But of course! I am too selfish to allow you to have any. Besides, I think it would be very bad for you. You are a great deal too fond of having your own way, my lord.'

He smiled and let that pass, thinking it wise to change the subject. 'Well, ma'am, and has my aunt spoken to you of her plan for your immediate future?'

Eugenie looked mulish. 'She has, and I must tell you, my lord, that I am not to be so taken in. It is not her plan, but yours. What need have I of two months in the country? I do not wish to leave London, when I have only just arrived. And I do not like to have good done to me against my will.'

'Yes, you did warn me you were stubborn,' St Osyth grinned. 'But you do need rest, and you cannot do anything in Town with a broken leg which you could not do down at Freed. As for leaving London, everyone will be leaving soon for the summer – you cannot imagine how quiet and dull it will be when all the families have left for the country! I myself will be going down to Freed in August, as I always do.' He gauged the light in her eye, and added, 'Besides, you would be doing the greatest kindness to Lady Mary in submitting. She loves Freed so, but she will not go down there on her own account. You would be giving her both the excuse and the company.'

She eyed him askance. 'Oh, you are clever, Lord St Osyth, very clever.'

'And for amusement you shall choose your own company,' he added persuasively. 'Only tell me whom you wish to see, and I shall invite them all to Freed as a house party.'

'Even your cousin Sebastian?' she asked quickly.

'Even he,' the Earl agreed blandly.

'And poor Mr Martin?'

'I have already offered him the same opportunity for convalescence,' he said. 'But you need not fear that you will lose touch with your rescuer. I am in need of a new confidential secretary, and Mr Thomas Martin has accepted the position.'

'Oh, how glad I am,' Eugenie said warmly. 'That is a benevolence which will benefit you both.'

'I am sure of it,' said St Osyth. 'At all events, he will be able to use the time at Freed to acquaint himself with the details of my estate and my business, so you will certainly see him there. And whom else shall I ask for you?'

Her face took on a shining innocence. 'What if I asked for Mr and Mrs McKendrick? What would you say then?'

'That I owe them both a great deal,' St Osyth smiled. 'Why should I refuse to have them at Freed?'

'And Mrs Holland Burrage?'

'If you want her, you shall have her,' he said unperturbed.

'Oh, you are a great deal too good to live!' cried Eugenie. 'I cannot argue with an angel. To Freed I shall go!'

Chapter Thirteen

Eugenie might protest, but once the difficulties and discomforts of the journey were over, she was very glad to be at Freed. The experiences she had endured had left her nerves and spirits sorely tried, and she was in need of the rest and recuperation which only the regenerative peace of the countryside could supply. The first morning that she woke in the pretty, modern chamber which Mrs Bacon had had prepared for her, and heard no sound from without but bird song and the gentle rustling of the breeze in the creeper around her window, she felt the first premonitions of a great happiness.

The house was neither very large nor very old, though the land had belonged to the Freeds since Plantagenet days. Lady Mary's grandfather had pulled down the old house – a part-mediaeval, part-Tudor building, rambling, draughty and inconvenient – and built instead a jewel of a Palladian mansion, neat, symmetrical, and elegant. It was faced in Portland stone and decorated with a very pretty creeper, and had such modern appurtenances of a broad terrace commanding magnificent views, neat formal gardens and pretty walks, as would most benefit the weary spirits of a young woman with a broken leg.

Lord St Osyth had sent word ahead of Eugenie for a wheeled chair to be acquired for her use, a thoughtfulness for which she was most grateful, for it meant that with

Marie to push her she was free to move about the ground floor of the house and the upper levels of the gardens and terraces without need of a footman's attendance. For the first week, she was happy just to sit in the sun and gaze at the sweet, burgeoning scenes of the English countryside all around her, and to absorb the nourishment which Mrs Bacon eagerly provided at regular intervals. Fresh food from the home farm – eggs, milk and cheese from the dairy in addition to an extraordinary array of fruits from the kitchen garden, orchard and succession houses – all were placed before her with an anxious, searching look, and supplemented by bottles of the finest wine, brought up from the cellar by the ancient butler, Egret: 'On his lordship's specific orders, my lady. I was to be sure your ladyship drunk at least a glass at every meal.'

Eugenie had a great deal to occupy her thoughts. Since her arrival in England so much had happened so rapidly that she had not had time to reflect, to adjust her thoughts to her new life. Tante Alicie's execution, Papa's death, her flight from her homeland, her loss, in exile, of all she had possessed – these things had to be pondered over, so that they could take their proper places in her memory. Great ill fortune had been followed by great good luck in her finding, in Lady Mary, a new family and a new home. Though she was now a penniless dependant, Lady Mary was at great pains to ensure she never felt it, and nothing could have been more kind than her treatment, nothing more respectful than the attitudes of the servants. Yet she must regret the loss of that independence which her birth and fortune had given her, and mourn the terrible events in France which had robbed her of her home, and which were daily causing the world to recoil in horror from her fellow countrymen as savage barbarians.

As her weary nerves healed themselves and her strength and spirits grew, there was plenty to occupy her. The Earls of St Osyth had over a number of generations built up an impressive library of books which was at her disposal, and if England was to be her new home, Eugenie felt it became her to absorb its literature. There was Lady Mary to talk to, a Lady Mary made wonderfully high-spirited by her return to her childhood home, which she had always dearly loved. She liked to tell Eugenie stories of her childhood, and sat for hours chatting to her while Eugenie and Marie stitched at the first of a series of new gowns they had promised her.

And there was Thomas Martin who, once he had recovered from his concussion, made a lively and amusing companion, one whose cheerful volubility ensured that the ladies were never dull. He had the work of the estate to learn, but he had also developed such a strongly protective partiality for Eugenie's company, that he could never be away long without returning to see if she wanted something fetched, or her chair moved. He liked to tell her all the things he had discovered since she last saw him, and in that way Eugenie learned almost as much about the estate as he did. He made an indefatigable audience for Lady Mary's reminiscences, and in the evenings invented a series of perfectly foolish games for them to play, which kept them in fits of laughter.

He was more than grateful to the Earl for offering him the position of confidential secretary, for it was an advancement which made any number of other careers in the future a possibility. Eugenie discovered that he nursed a hitherto secret desire to enter Parliament, something which previously had seemed so unlikely an achievement that he had never spoken of it to anyone. But from private secretary to the richest earl in England, the step was not nearly so large, and when he was alone with Eugenie, he spoke eagerly of it as though it were a thing certain to happen one day.

So her time passed very easily and pleasantly as her broken bone knitted. The surgeon from Leicester who was called in to attend her pronounced himself very satisfied with her progress, and said that a complete recovery with no after-effects could confidently be looked for in the course of time. Why, then, did she experience an occasional flatness of spirits, and why did her mind continually wander to the thought of the beginning of August, as though that date were to bring about some improvement to her situation? Marie, watching her out of the corner of her eye, sometimes sighed and sometimes smiled at her mistress's preoccupation, and confided in Thomas Martin, with whom she had become great friends, that the attempted kidnap may have done some harm that was not yet apparent.

The Earl was expected towards the end of the first week in August, but when the ladies went down to breakfast on the thirtieth of July they found his lordship already sitting at the table, talking to Martin and addressing a large plate of buttered eggs, delicately sliced ham and lamb cutlets, while Egret, smiling as though his face would fall in two, eagerly refilled his coffee cup.

'My dear Max, how delightful to see you! And before you were looked for, too!' Lady Mary cried, stepping forward. St Osyth rose from his seat wiping his mouth, and came round the table to embrace his aunt; but his eyes went inexorably past her to where Eugenie sat in her wheeled chair in the doorway, her cheeks, which had paled at the sight of him, now unaccountably rosy. Their eyes met, and he came forward to shake hands with her.

'My dear ma'am, I hope I find you much improved? Thomas tells me that you have been going along tolerably well. He has been keeping you entertained, I understand?'

'Thank you, yes,' said Eugenie, her hand still in his. 'The surgeon is very pleased with me, and everything has been done for my comfort. I have lacked for nothing here.' But her eyes, fixed on his face, belied her statement, and she made no attempt to release her fingers from his warm grasp.

St Osyth, smiling a dismissal to Marie, took over charge of the chair and wheeled Eugenie to the table.

'But where is Sebastian, St Osyth?' Lady Mary asked. 'I thought he was to accompany you when you came down.'

'He will follow in a week or so, ma'am. I came early for a particular reason. I have some news which I was anxious to impart without delay.' He sat down beside Eugenie and gathered her full attention. 'It is news from France, ma'am. Robespierre is dead. He was overthrown from power two days since, tried, and executed. The Terror is over – it is all over. Robespierre is no more.'

Eugenie gazed at him, her eyes wide, and then with a little cry she put her face into her hands. 'Thank God!' she said, and wept.

Now that the Earl was in residence, the pace of the house increased. There were comings and goings all day, and the silence was continually disturbed by sounds of arrival, footsteps, voices and laughter, the housebell ringing. Neighbours, friends and tenants called to pay their respects to his lordship as soon as they saw the standard raised on the flagpole over the front pediment of the house. Agents, stewards and gamekeepers had reports to make and questions to ask. Invitations were issued and accepted, guests engaged for dinner, and extra servants hired to supply the increased needs of the house.

Thomas Martin was at the Earl's elbow whenever there was business to attend to, and St Osyth did not learn to regret his choice of secretary: Martin was intelligent, quick-witted, diligent, painstaking, and rapidly displayed an ability to act on his own initiative which delighted the Earl and earned him praise. Both of them were so occupied that the ladies saw little of them until the evening. Why then, Marie asked herself rhetorically, was her mistress so much more cheerful than before? Why did she sing in her bath, and choose her gown for dinner with so much more concentration?

The news from France continued to be good. The Terror was definitely over: a more moderate form of government had ensued, and thousands of prisoners, who had been awaiting the certain death of the guillotine, had been released. Eugenie waited, hardly daring to hope, for news of her missing servants. If they were not dead, surely they would write to her? She waited impatiently every morning for the footman to return with the letters, but on the tenth of August an excited servant came running to fetch Eugenie and Marie to the great hall where, instead of a letter, she found Nana and Pierre themselves, looking very bewildered and weary from travel, in the charge of Sebastian, who was grinning with delight.

'See what I have brought you! Is not this a famous surprise?' he said as soon as he saw Eugenie, but he managed to say no more before the sound of his voice was drowned by the cries of the French servants as they saw their beloved mistress at last. There were exclamations and tears of joy, kissings and huggings and explanations, and it was a long time before Sebastian could tell his part of the story.

'They went to Brompton to try to find you there, and some friend of your maidservant sent them on to Berrington House,' he told Eugenie, who had already heard a tangled version of it in French. 'Old Treese couldn't understand what they were saying, but supposed it must be something to do with you, and decided the best thing was to send for me. Thank heaven I had not left London! Of course, my French isn't so very wonderful, but it didn't take a great deal of intelligence to understand that they were the two servants you had mislaid. I hope you are pleased with them. They must have a dashed interesting tale to tell.'

Eugenie, between tears and hugs, astonishment and delight, found it difficult to supply her tongue with words in the correct language, and found it easier to rely for the first half-hour or so on smiles and nods. But old Nana had some important news, which she was eager to impart at the first opportunity.

'The leather trunk, my lady – the one you entrusted to

us – we have it safe, my lady. It is there, in the corner. Pierre would not let it out of his sight for an instant. You had better take it, my lady, and make sure all is well.'

Eugenie stared, her eyes enormous. 'My jewels? You managed to save my jewels?'

'Yes, my lady,' Pierre said, matter-of-factly. 'When we found Abbeville full of gendarmes, we took a long way round to avoid them, but we couldn't get to St Omer, not without passing them. So we stopped in a wood by the road, and I buried the trunk, good and deep, under a tree, before we went on. They stopped us all right, and questioned us, and when we wouldn't tell them anything, they put us in prison, and there we've stayed all this time.'

'Lucky we were to be there, my lady, from all we've heard,' Nana said grimly. 'They were executing the folk in Paris by the thousand, so we heard. Well, as soon as the Old Spider was done away with, they opened up the prisons and let us all out, so Pierre and me, we went back and dug up the trunk and went on to St Omer, as we'd been told.' She looked apologetic. 'We had to sell something, my lady, to buy our passage on the boat. I sold those diamond earrings you never liked. I didn't know what to do for the best.'

Eugenie hugged her again, laughing through tears at all they had endured for her sake. 'Oh foolish Nana, did you think I'd be cross? I am so glad to see you both again! I never thought you would bring me my fortune as well!'

'Well, this is good news indeed,' the Earl said as he pushed Eugenie in her chair through the formal gardens towards what had become a favourite spot of hers, a little white stone temple in the Greek style from which one could see the whole layout of the walks. 'From what you tell me, you have become a wealthy woman again.'

'Yes,' she said contentedly. 'Not so wealthy as I was in France, but I have my independence again, and that is the best.'

'Was it irksome, to be Lady Mary's protégée?'

'Lady Mary is kindness itself, and I love her dearly. But to have an independence is to be free – to have choice. It changes everything.'

He reached the temple, turned her chair to face the view, and sat down on a little stone bench where he could see her face. 'Yes,' he said. 'It changes everything.' She glanced at him, and met his eyes, and was forced to look away, her cheeks burning. 'There is something I wish to talk to you about,' he said.

'Indeed, my lord?'

'Indeed, ma'am. When I found you at last, in the woods, after having thought for so many hours that I should never see you again, I realised that you had become very dear to me. Eugenie – allow me to call you by that name, for it is what I call you in my private thoughts, always!'

'Indeed, my lord,' she said again, dimpling.

'Indeed – how you like that word! And how you like to torment me with pretending you don't know what I am trying to say!'

'Oh, you are managing very well, my lord. Pray continue,' she said demurely. 'I am all attention.'

'Minx!' he apostrophised her. 'Do you pretend not to know that I am very much in love with you?'

'*Tiens!* That is very interesting,' she said, eyes wide. 'And is this a declaration?'

'Yes, it is a declaration, you provoking child! You may wonder why I did not declare myself to you at once, for I am sure I said and did enough then to convince you that you must expect it. But I did not wish to add to the strain upon your nerves at a time when you were exhausted from your experiences. I wanted you to have time to recover, so that you might receive my offer with a calm mind.'

'A Frenchwoman must always be calm, my lord, when receiving an offer of marriage,' she said with an impish grin. 'It is a very serious business. But tell me, why did you say nothing when you arrived here at Freed, and saw that I was well and happy?'

He hesitated. 'You may think it foolish, but it was for the very reason that you were dependant, that you had no fortune and no freedom. I was afraid that if I offered for you, you might scruple to accept me, penniless as you were.'

'Oh no, you mistake,' she said pleasantly. 'I am not so nice! You are in more danger now, for now that I have my fortune again, I am free to refuse you, if I wish.'

St Osyth jumped up in exasperation. 'You will go too far, ma'am, in teasing me,' he cried, and as she laughed gleefully, he knelt beside her chair so as to take her hands in his and look into her eyes. 'Eugenie, please tell me,' he said seriously. 'Am I mistaken? Have I misread the signs? I love you with all my heart – do you love me?'

Her dark eyes shone, and her lips curved into a delicious smile. 'You are not mistaken,' she said, and was clasped immediately to him, while he murmured distracted endearments in her ear, releasing her only sufficiently to kiss her fervently upon the lips, an embrace she returned with great interest. When she was free to speak again, she said, 'But I have not yet said I will marry you.'

He released her as if stung, and scowled at her. 'Now what?' he demanded tersely.

'I must tell you that there is one great impediment to our marriage, my lord,' she said gravely.

'Which is?' he asked impatiently.

'That you have never apologised to me for splashing me with your curricle. I cannot marry you unless you do so.'

St Osyth resumed his seat at a little distance from her and regarded her carefully. 'Now, Eugenie, you cannot be serious.'

'Indeed I am,' she said. 'How could you respect me, if I were to give up such an important point?'

The idea of respecting her had not occurred to him, and

he frowned over it. 'But could you respect *me*, if I gave in to you?' he demanded.

'That is a very good question,' she said seriously. 'I had not considered it. Now, I wonder how we can resolve this problem? You are determined not to apologise to me, which makes you very stubborn, almost as stubborn as I am. It would be very bad for you to have your own way once again – and yet I would not have you yield, for I like you as you are, though you have very grave faults of character.'

His eyes gleamed. 'You consider that I need a reforming influence upon me?'

'Without a doubt,' she replied in kind.

'Then, my dear Eugenie, you must certainly marry me, for as my wife you would have so much more influence over me than you can ever hope to have as Lady Mary's protégée!'

'In that case,' she said, giving him an entirely different smile, which brought him to her side again, 'purely for your own good, I must accept you.'

'Purely for my sake?' he murmured, kissing her again. But Eugenie, wrapped in his arms, was too busy establishing her influence over him to reply.